Other Books By Marc D. Hasbrouck

MURDER ON THE STREET OF YEARS
DOWN WITH THE SUN
STABLE AFFAIRS
HORSE SCENTS

REMEMBER YOU MUST DIE

Marc D. Hasbrouck

REMEMBER YOU MUST DIE

Copyright © 2022 Marc D. Hasbrouck.

All rights reserved. No part of this book may be used or reproduced by any means, graphic, electronic, or mechanical, including photocopying, recording, taping or by any information storage retrieval system without the written permission of the author except in the case of brief quotations embodied in critical articles and reviews.

Certain characters in this work are historical figures, and certain events portrayed did take place. However, this is a work of fiction. All of the other characters, names, and events as well as all places, incidents, organizations, and dialogue in this novel are either the products of the author's imagination or are used fictitiously.

iUniverse books may be ordered through booksellers or by contacting:

iUniverse
1663 Liberty Drive
Bloomington, IN 47403
www.iuniverse.com
844-349-9409

Because of the dynamic nature of the Internet, any web addresses or links contained in this book may have changed since publication and may no longer be valid. The views expressed in this work are solely those of the author and do not necessarily reflect the views of the publisher, and the publisher hereby disclaims any responsibility for them.

Any people depicted in stock imagery provided by Getty Images are models, and such images are being used for illustrative purposes only. Certain stock imagery © Getty Images.

Author's Photo Credit: Gaylin E. Hasbrouck

ISBN: 978-1-6632-4368-3 (sc)
ISBN: 978-1-6632-4367-6 (e)

Library of Congress Control Number: 2022915607

Print information available on the last page.

iUniverse rev. date: 08/19/2022

Vita brevis breviter in brevi finietur,
Mors venit velociter quae neminem veretur,
Omnia mors perimit et nulli miseretur.
Ad mortem festinamus peccare desistamus.

Life is short, and shortly it will end;
Death comes quickly and respects no one,
Death destroys everything and takes pity on no one.
To death we are hastening, let us refrain from sinning.

From the virelai *ad mortem festinamus*
of the Llibre Vermell de Montserrat, 1399

A Brief Word from the Author

I had so much fun creating and writing about the fictitious London-based author Devon Stone in my previous book, *Murder On The Street Of Years*, that I decided to pay him and some of his friends a return visit. Along with Devon, we find that Veronica Barron, Billy Bennett, and Peyton Chase get themselves wrapped up in another perilous tale and soon discover that murder is an art. *Murder On The Street Of Years* dealt with the hatred remaining following World War II and some of its ramifications. All the murders within that book were revenge murders, justified or otherwise. That decision of justification I shall leave to my readers.

As if it were written during the mid-1950s, I have approached the storyline in *this* book from a different angle. A highly classified mission during World War II is a mere bit player, playing a supporting role in this drama…but a pivotal one. This is a story about coincidences, happenstance, and serendipity, if you will. What happens with chance encounters and their consequences have always intrigued me. Being in the wrong place at the right time, or being in the right place at the wrong time. Or being in the wrong place at the wrong time. I take this theme to the extreme here. Some people might think that there are no such things as coincidences. Everything happens for a reason. Perhaps. Again, I leave that for my readers to decide.

But in *this* case, happenstance just happens to lead to murder. Several of them.

And, as in my previous book, Devon Stone's hyperthymesia comes into play within the following pages. This syndrome is a very real one and was only diagnosed as recently as 2006. The actress Marilu Henner is one of only twelve people currently worldwide who have been diagnosed with it. It is also known as Superior Autobiographical Memory.

There will be factual historical information relating to my story at the end of this book in the Author's Notes. Aside from learning a little tidbit about World War II, you might be surprised to learn about a section of New York City with a tragic and deadly history.

I hope you enjoy reading this book as much as I enjoyed writing it.

Let's begin!

PART ONE
FASTEN YOUR SEATBELTS

*"Flying might not be all plain sailing, but
the fun of it is worth the price."*

———

AMELIA EARHART

Prologue

June 2, 1953
The Contract Expires

"Don't come any closer," she said, almost trembling.

As he made a step toward her, she raised the pistol. That action made no difference. He smiled and took another step. He couldn't ever imagine that she would actually shoot him.

He was mistaken.

He reached out toward her and she fired. She watched in horror as the red blotch grew on his chest, oozing through his thin shirt. He staggered, shocked, backward out the open door. The railing to the balcony behind him didn't stop his movement. He couldn't stop the momentum and he disappeared over it, falling the three flights to the floor of the lobby below where his skull cracked open, splattering blood and brain matter.

She ran to the railing, looked down, and saw him lying there, contorted, motionless on the white marble floor surrounded by a widening pool of blood. Not believing that she had really and truly shot him, still brandishing her gun she blindly ran down the spiraling steps of the four-sided stairwell stopping only when she breathlessly reached the last step. She burst through the door into the lobby and stood there in shock and confusion.

A gun was pointed squarely at her chest.

1

Two Months Earlier

Following the announcement by the stewardess, Devon Stone brought his seat back to the full upright position and made sure his seatbelt was securely fastened. He glanced out of his first-class window as the BOAC Lockheed Constellation made a wide circle making its final descent into Idlewild Airport in New York. In the distance he saw the lights of the Manhattan skyscrapers start to come on and twinkle in the early spring evening. Despite the comfort of first-class, and several walks up and down the aisle over the past few hours, Devon was eager to stretch his six-foot, two frame. Upon takeoff from London, he had been pleasantly surprised when he realized that the seat next to him would remain empty for the flight. He had been even more surprised when he saw that there were only five other passengers in first-class. Three men and two women.

Less than one hour after their departure from London nearly half a day earlier, a fellow passenger in the first-class cabin made a discovery. She was reading the latest murder mystery from her favorite author. *The Fallen* was a somewhat vivid and, at times, violent story about revenge. She didn't necessarily buy into revenge as a justifiable reason for murder. She closed the book and turned it over in her lap. She glanced at the full color photograph of the very handsome Devon Stone on the back cover and gasped. She turned to look at that very same gentleman sitting across the aisle from her just as the stewardess was handing him a gin and tonic. He raised the glass as in silent toast, winked at the stewardess, and sensed that he was being watched. He turned and caught the eye of the reader across the aisle.

He glanced at the book that was still overturned on her lap. He raised his glass once again and winked at her.

"Are you flirting with me, young man?" chuckled the woman. She was only slightly overweight, dressed in the latest of fashions, and probably no younger than seventy.

"I was just admiring your reading material," answered Devon Stone. "Shocking, isn't it?" he laughed.

"Well," she replied, "I *am* a bit shocked, honestly, by the murders for revenge. Goes against my nature. I'm assuming it must go against yours as well. But, as the author, you write what sells, don't you?" as she winked right back at him.

Devon Stone chuckled to himself. One must *never* assume.

"Please excuse my brazenness, Mr. Stone," she said as she stretched her hand across the aisle, "I'm Brenda Barratt. I guess I wasn't paying attention when I boarded and I never even noticed you sitting there. I do need new glasses, though. Can hardly see anything more than five feet in front of me. Well, that's a slight exaggeration. But only slight. It never dawned on me that I'd have such an esteemed author practically in my lap, so to speak."

Devon Stone shook her hand and hers was a firm handshake at that. "A pleasure to meet you, Brenda," he replied.

"All my friends call me B.B.," she said with a chuckle, "just like the gun. I don't suppose you'd be kind enough to autograph my book…well, your book…for me, would you?"

"I thought you'd never ask," Devon responded with a wide smile. He reached into his jacket pocket for a pen as she handed the book to him. He thought about it for a second, and then inscribed the title page to her.

Dearest B.B.
Revenge can be sweet
Devon Stone
2/4/1953

He handed the book back to her and she glanced at the inscription, shaking her head and smiling as she did so. She glanced at the photograph on the back cover again and then, holding it up, she compared the photo with the real person.

"I must say that the photograph doesn't do you justice, Mr. Stone. You're *much* better-looking…and younger looking, as well. You certainly have that Cary Grant thing going, don't you?"

"Are *you* flirting with *me*, young lady?" Devon chuckled.

"Perhaps. A little. Old ladies have that privilege. If you don't mind my asking, Mr. Stone, what brings you to the States?"

"A bit of business and a smattering of research for my next book. I'm nearly ready to send one to the publisher now and I've started on yet another that will be partly set in Manhattan. Actually I'm here to meet with my American publisher to set up a book tour. And I have to meet with some of their lawyers."

"Oh, be wary of our American lawyers," said B.B. with a sigh. "They can be a shady, shrewd lot, can't they? My beloved father once told me to keep skunks, bankers, and lawyers at a distance. He encountered all three unfortunately. I, too, will be meeting with one of those shady lawyers in a couple days. Some ugly old family business to attend to. I wish my husband were still alive to handle the ordeal. Nasty. Oh, well. On a different note, where will you be staying?"

"Not that I come to the States that often anymore," answered Devon Stone, "but I always stay at the old renowned Algonquin. Love that old place. I keep hoping to encounter the ghosts from the infamous Round Table. Fellow writers, you know."

"Oh, yes, I remember reading about that group," B.B. said. "I would have loved being a fly on the wall with that motley bunch. Critics, writers, and actors with rapier wits. And all of them probably drunk, at that!"

"Oh, I have no doubt," responded Devon Stone. "That would have been half the fun!"

They both chuckled.

"And you, B.B.? I assume that you're heading home now, right?" asked Devon.

"I've been visiting some old friends and my sister in your beautiful city, Mr. Stone. Some of it was pleasant. Some of it was definitely *not*, sadly. Yes, I'm heading home. I live in New Jersey but I'm staying a couple nights in Manhattan. I'm meeting someone for a late dinner this evening at the Plaza, where I'll be staying. Then I'll see a couple shows on

Broadway for the next few nights and I do need to stop in at the Museum of Modern Art."

"I have a couple of acquaintances who live in New Jersey," replied Devon. "I don't know if I'll have the chance to see them or not. Do you know of a town called Dover?"

B.B. laughed.

"Goodness, small world, isn't it? Yes, I know Dover very well. My family has lived there for generations. I actually live not too far from there now, in Morristown. The reason I'm meeting with a lawyer has to do with some dealings in Dover. I won't bother you with the details. Too boring."

She closed her eyes and leaned back in her seat, inhaling deeply. Devon thought she might be getting ill or on the verge of passing out.

"I'm sorry to have disturbed your flight, Mr. Stone. I have a tendency to get airsick when I fly and I guess the Dramamine is finally kicking in. It's making me quite drowsy. I enjoyed our little chat and thank you, so much, for your autograph. I shall cherish it forever. Good luck with your lawyers and book tour."

Devon was momentarily concerned but the lady seemed to drift off into a peaceful sleep. When the stewardess came along with the food cart for a mid-flight luncheon, Brenda Barratt politely declined, covered her lap with a blanket, and resumed her slumber. Devon also declined the meal, but enjoyed two more gin and tonics before nodding off himself. He was awakened by the announcement regarding the imminent arrival at their destination.

As the plane steadied itself for the final approach to landing, Devon glanced across the aisle to see that Brenda Barratt was alert once again and gathering her things. He watched as she scribbled a short note and stuck it into the book, *The Fallen*, which Devon had signed.

Devon's ears popped as the plane descended faster while making a shallow 90-degree turn and aligning with the runway. Swooping in over Jamaica Bay, the wheels touched down to a smattering of applause from the passengers in coach.

The propellers slowed and the plane almost silently taxied to their awaiting gate. Devon reached down to put his shoes back on and tie them. The Fasten Seatbelt sign dinged off and he turned to say goodbye to B.B. but by then the aisle was filled with passengers eager to deplane following the long flight and she was already gone. Retrieving his attaché case from the overhead compartment, he joined the other travelers as they headed into the terminal and to the international arrivals baggage claim. He looked for her as they slowly moved through customs. She must have beaten him there obviously and had been swiftly cleared.

Spry old lady, he thought to himself, shrugging his shoulders. Passport stamped, he collected his small piece of luggage and headed to the taxi stands outside, ready to head into the city.

2

Brenda Barratt tipped the bellhop handsomely as he placed her suitcase on the folding stand just inside her hotel room door.

"Welcome to the Plaza, ma'am," he said. "We hope you enjoy your stay."

He bowed slightly as he thanked her and handed her the room key. She turned and noticed an unusually large bouquet of yellow roses almost overpowering a small table in the middle of the room. *How odd*, she thought, *what are those for and from whom?*

Brenda Barratt loved roses and knew the meaning behind each color. Yellow roses, for example, are the color of friendship. But, on the other hand, she also knew that in the Victorian era yellow roses actually represented jealousy. So which were these?

There was a business-sized envelope propped up against the base of the vase holding the flowers. She put on her reading glasses and picked up the envelope, turning it over to see if there was anything written on either side. There was not. She carefully tore it open and extracted the single sheet of beautiful onionskin paper. Centered on the page, halfway between the top and bottom, were two typewritten words.

She was instantly seething. "Those bastards," she said letting the words hiss through her teeth.

After unpacking a few things, she pulled open a drawer on the small desk in her room. Finding some hotel stationery, she wrote a note, sealed the envelope and called down to the front desk. A few moments later the same bellhop knocked on her door and she handed him the envelope along with a request and a ten-dollar bill.

Twenty minutes later there was a slight knock on her door, which startled her. *Perhaps the bellhop again with a question,* she thought. She certainly wasn't expecting anyone. Although she had told Devon Stone that she was meeting a friend for dinner, she remembered on the taxi ride from the airport that the dinner date was for tomorrow night, not tonight. *Oh, well*, she thought, *Devon Stone has probably forgotten all about it anyway. Nor would he even care.*

Brenda Barratt set Devon Stone's book with her brief scribbled note tucked inside it on the table next to the roses. She looked through the peephole in her door and then stood back, confused and conflicted. Opening her hotel room door, she glared at who was standing there.

"But…" she said.

Devon Stone checked into the Algonquin and was ushered up to his spacious one-bedroom suite by a somewhat annoying and talkative bellhop. *The bloke is obviously hoping for a decent tip*, thought Devon, listening patiently as they entered his room.

"Here long, are ya, Mr. Stone?" asked the bellhop as he placed Devon's suitcase on a folding stand by the entryway. "Do ya like shows? If you're interested, my kid brother is a singer and dancer in that great show *Wonderful Town* and I can get ya some good seats. I seen it three times already and it's a hoot, I ain't kiddin' ya!"

Devon rolled his eyes at the grammar and tried to be as polite as possible.

"I appreciate the offer, my good man, but musicals, hoot or otherwise, curdle my blood. No offense, I hope, to your brother or anyone else involved. *But*, on the other hand, if someone gets murdered in it, I might change my mind. Anyone get their throats slit in this show, by any chance?"

The bellhop stood silently.

"Uhh, no, sir," was his solemn and barely whispered reply. "I don't think anyone would *ever* want to see a musical with folks getting their throats slit. Even here in New York."

"Oh, well," answered Devon Stone shrugging his shoulders. "Thanks anyway, but I'll pass on the offer, a hoot or otherwise."

He handed the bellhop three crisp, new one-dollar bills and wished him a friendly goodnight as he closed the hotel room door.

His publisher, knowing Devon Stone only too well, had made sure that a new, large bottle of Gordon's Gin was waiting for him in the suite's living room. Devon chuckled when he saw it, and read the welcoming note: *Cheers! Both you and Hemingway have great taste. Enjoy!*

A few minutes later he glanced at the room service menu and placed a call ordering his dinner along with several bottles of tonic and plenty of ice. His publisher was picking up the tab, so let's go big. It was a difficult decision but he settled on the eight-ounce Porcini Crusted Filet Mignon served with creamed spinach, and tri-color fingerling sautéed in foie gras butter. By the time his order was delivered to his door, he had changed into his pajamas and wrapped the fluffy hotel-supplied robe around himself.

As he ate (and drank) he reviewed several notes that he wanted to cover with his American publisher. He also worked on some revisions for his latest manuscript that he had thought about while on the flight from London. He thought he might call over to the Plaza Hotel to chat with Brenda Barratt to learn a bit more about her troubling situation, but then he remembered that she was meeting a friend for dinner and changed his mind.

Two hours later, with a full stomach and a half-empty bottle of Gordon's, his eyes were beginning to droop and he decided to call it a night and go to bed.

3

Still being on London time, Devon Stone lay tossing and turning wide-awake in his comfortable bed at the Algonquin at 3 A.M. And still at 4 A.M. By 5:30 he decided to get up, take a long hot bath and then go down to the dining room for a very early breakfast. The warm water was so relaxing that he leaned back in the tub and finally fell asleep. He was jolted awake by the ringing of his telephone. Stepping from the now-cold tub and wrapping a towel around his waist, he glanced at his watch.

"Well, I'll be damned," he exclaimed to himself. It was now 8 A.M.

"Good morning, Mr. Stone," chirped the friendly voice as Devon answered. "I hope we didn't disturb you too early but there is someone in the lobby who needs to speak with you."

"I'm not expecting anyone, miss, did he…or she…say what they want?"

"It's a he, Mr. Stone. No, he didn't tell me what he wants but it's a police officer."

Devon Stone sighed and thought about that statement for the briefest of seconds.

"I need to get dressed, young lady. Please tell him to give me five minutes and then send him up to my room."

"Yes, Mr. Stone. Thank you." And the call ended.

This trip might be a bit more of an adventure than I imagined, Devon thought to himself. But why in blazes would a police officer be calling on him at the crack of dawn?

Devon was dressed and waiting before the knock came on his door. Whoever it was had waited fifteen minutes. Without looking through the security peephole, he cautiously opened the door. Standing before him was a tall dark-haired man, looking to be in his late thirties or early forties, wearing a dapper dark navy blue serge suit, white shirt with spearpoint collars, fronted by a striking navy and white necktie with a small houndstooth pattern tied with a perfect Windsor knot. Devon was momentarily taken aback by this example of sartorial splendor. Certainly *not* what he was expecting. The man smiled.

"Devon Stone?" asked the good-looking young gentleman. "I hate to bother you but we have a bit of a nasty situation that needs attention."

He turned, looking up and down the hotel hallway.

"I'm sorry for the intrusion but may I step inside?"

There was an awkward silence for a few seconds.

"Oh, bloody hell, yes, of course, young man. I'm sorry myself for not asking you to step in. I just arrived in town late last night and I'm somewhat taken aback by a policeman calling on me almost immediately. I assume that you *are*, indeed, the policeman of whom the hotel clerk alerted me? I expected to see a uniformed officer."

The man chuckled and held out a badge and identification for Devon to inspect as he stepped into the room. Devon slowly closed the door behind him.

"I'm James Lafferty, sir, a detective. And, before we go any further, I am indeed privileged to meet you Mr. Stone. I am an avid reader and you are just about my favorite."

"Well, then," answered Devon with a broad smile, "It is *I* who is privileged to be *just about your favorite*. But let's cut to the chase, Detective Lafferty. I have not been in the city long enough to cause any altercation of any kind. The only other person I've confronted before arriving at the hotel was the unruly cabbie who tried to take me the longest way here from the airport. Trust me, he learned a few new words as a result."

James Lafferty laughed.

"Your humor is just as pointed in person as on the printed page, Mr. Stone. You're a hoot."

Devon Stone stared at him. Hoot. There's that phrase again.

"I'm assuming by *hoot* you don't mean that I sound like an owl. Or the honking of a car horn?"

"No, sir, I'm sorry. That might be an Americanism. I meant no disrespect."

Devon laughed.

"Relax, I'm just pulling your leg, lad. Or is *that* another Americanism?"

The detective looked embarrassed but quickly regained his composure.

"But this is somber business we're now dealing with, I'm afraid. Do you know a Brenda Barratt, Mr. Stone?"

"I do not *know* Brenda Barratt, but I *do* know to whom you are referring," answered Devon Stone.

"Care to elaborate on that?" asked the now serious detective.

"She was a fellow passenger on my flight from London yesterday. We introduced ourselves and had a brief chat. Why? What's the problem?"

"Well, she must have known you and you her before then. I saw the book that you autographed to her back in February, so you must have known her before yesterday's flight."

"February?" asked an incredulous Devon Stone. "What do you mean February?"

The Inspector opened his small note pad and showed Devon the date from the inscription: *2/4/1953.*

Devon smiled, shaking his head. "You Americans can never get things correct can you? The date for example. You write it all wrong. Evidently you write month, day and then the year. We Brits write the day first, then the month and then the year. I did, indeed, autograph her book but it *was* yesterday. At 11:32 A.M. still on London time and at approximately 25,000 feet somewhere over the Atlantic. I swear."

"Oh," answered Lafferty sheepishly. "Well, then. Okay, but she had a note tucked into that book as well. It simply read *Devon Stone, Algonquin.* That's how we found you here. We just played a hunch and it was correct."

"And so, as I said a few moments ago, young man, let's cut to the chase once again. Why have you had to play a hunch and track me down? I've done nothing wrong that I know of. Did I offend her in some way? Signing an autograph isn't even a misdemeanor."

"I *shall* cut to the chase, as you ask. Brenda Barratt was savagely murdered last night. In her hotel room."

Devon Stone inhaled quickly and sat down abruptly on the closest chair.

"Good lord, man, that's ghastly. I'm stunned. I…I don't know what else to say."

The detective waited a moment or two as he watched Devon's pained expression.

"Alongside of your book in her room was a note with two simple words written on it. Well, typed on it. At this point, I have no idea what those words mean. Do you have any idea what this means?"

James Lafferty held up his notebook with the two words written in it. Devon read them.

"Yes, I *do* know what that means," he answered.

"And how do you know that, Mr. Stone?"

"I'm a writer and I know things. *Memento Mori*. It's Latin."

"And it means exactly what, sir?"

"It means *Remember You Must Die.*

4

"I don't mean to be impertinent, sir, and please don't read anything into this, but you didn't seem to hesitate even for a moment when I asked if you knew Brenda Barratt," said James Lafferty. "You said that you had just met her on your flight and spoke to her briefly."

"You're a New Yorker, I assume," answered Devon. "Impertinence is an inherited trait here. Don't apologize for it. Embrace it. Regarding my lack of hesitation when you mentioned her name, I just happen to have a memory that's frightening."

"What do you mean by that? I don't understand."

"What I mean," replied Devon Stone with a sigh and a shoulder shrug, "is that I simply cannot forget *anything*. And I do mean anything. Ever. We need go no further with that."

The young detective gave Devon a slight frown along with *his* shoulder shrug.

"I'll have to take your word for that. I don't understand it, but I guess it's not my place to do so. So, Mr. Stone, in your brief conversation with the deceased did she happen to mention anything that might help in my investigation?"

"I can tell you *exactly* what we discussed and *exactly* what she said word for word but I'll be more concise. Before she fell asleep and dozed for most of the flight, she said that she was meeting a friend for a late dinner at her hotel. She was going to be attending several Broadway shows over the next few days and that she was to be meeting with some lawyers regarding some quote-unquote nasty business regarding something in Dover, New Jersey. She told me to be very wary of American lawyers. She was preaching to the choir with that one. I'm wary of *all* lawyers. Even dead ones."

James Flattery stared at Devon Stone for a brief moment or two.

"As far as that little note with my name and hotel is concerned…I haven't the foggiest notion as to why she would have it. Perhaps she wanted to contact me for some reason before she headed back home and noted where I was staying to remind herself. Obviously we'll never know about that one now."

"I noticed that your inscription to her in the book said that revenge could be sweet. That sounds a bit ominous to me, sir. What did you mean by that? And what kind of revenge?"

"Evidently you haven't read my latest book yet, have you? The one in question. *The Fallen*. It's about revenge killing and she didn't agree with the point of view of my protagonist. That's all. I was being flippant when I inscribed what I did. She assumed that I might agree with her and not have the capability of revenge or, more to the point, the capability of revenge killing."

"*Do* you have the capability of murder, Mr. Stone?"

Devon Stone smiled broadly and extended his arms outward, palms up.

"We *all* do, son, depending upon the situation. We all do. You're a New Yorker. You should understand."

"No, sir. I respectfully disagree with you, Mr. Stone. Yes, I'm a New Yorker but, no, I don't believe we are all…or can be…murderers depending upon the situation. I believe in common decency, accountability, morals, and the difference between right and wrong."

"There's a difference between the right thing and the legal thing, isn't there?" shrugged Devon.

"No, sir. There shouldn't be."

"Good lord, you're an imposter, aren't you Lafferty? Surely you can't be a true New Yorker?" said Stone winking.

"Now you're just pulling my leg again, aren't you, Mr. Stone? I mean, *really*."

Of course Devon Stone *had* committed murder. Perhaps they could be called revenge killings. But only a select few knew of it. He had dispatched a few contemptible and murderous Nazi sympathizers. He had no remorse. He planned to write a memoir many years into the future. It would be his final book, and he intended to make a full confession. But, at *that* time, he would demand his publisher to release the book no sooner than six months following his death.

Devon Stone smiled and shrugged his shoulders once again.

"I don't mean to be callous but, knowing my profession and also knowing that obviously I have no connection to Brenda Barratt's death in any way, could you please tell me how she was murdered? You initially told me savagely."

"Did I?"

"Don't question my memory, lad."

"Her throat was slashed. Practically from ear to ear. It must have been swift. No one heard any sounds of struggle or screaming for help. The maid for the turndown service found her around nine-thirty last evening. *Her* screams *were* heard. And the box along with her complementary mints were strewn everywhere in fright, as you can imagine."

"Hmm, interesting. No struggle you say. Obviously she must have opened her door feeling secure. We can assume, then," stated Devon Stone matter-of-factly, "that the killer was known to Miss Barratt."

"We? What's this *we*, Mr. Stone? You are being routinely interrogated, not being invited to help solve the crime."

"Only natural, dear boy, only natural. Please take no offense."

James Lafferty closed his little note pad and stood up to leave.

"Thank you for your time, Mr. Stone. I sincerely appreciate the information you have given me. I will have my department follow up on every detail. Oh, one more thing before I go. A heads-up, of sorts. The scavengers within the press followed me this morning. They obviously know who I am and what I do. Newspapers along with radio and TV stations are clamoring for as many vivid, lurid details as possible. That old quotation from William Randolph Hearst, *if it bleeds, it leads*, is the standard motto of the media, especially here in good old NYC. Don't be alarmed by what you see in the headlines later this morning. I, certainly, will divulge nothing of our visit here nor release your name but I cannot vouch for the clerks who work the front desk downstairs."

"I appreciate that, Detective James Lafferty. I do. Good luck with your investigation. I feel dreadful about poor Mrs. Barratt. She seemed like such a sweet elderly lady."

The detective was ushered out of the room and Devon suddenly felt tired. It was exhausting thinking about a horrendous murder. Calling his

17

publisher would have to wait. He emptied his bladder in the bathroom, and then collapsed onto his bed, falling into a long-awaited sleep.

Four hours later he was awakened by his telephone once again. He rolled over in bed, looked at his watch and groaned. He was still tired, more than slightly annoyed by the telephone ringing and now he was hungry as well. Reaching for the phone, he expected that it might be his publisher.

"Good afternoon, Mr. Stone," chirped that same friendly-sounding clerk at the front desk. "There are two gentlemen here in the lobby who want to see you as soon as possible."

"Are they either the press or more police?" asked Devon. He heard her turn away from the phone and ask the question. He heard no response. "No, sir, they are shaking their heads to both questions."

"Alright, then," said Devon, hoping these weren't the killer or killers coming to do him in. "Please send them up."

Less than five minutes later a loud knock came on his door. A *shave and a haircut two bits* kind of knock. He hesitated, and then he thrust open the door.

"Bloody hell!" he exclaimed.

Standing before him were Billy Bennett and Peyton Chase.

"What the *hell* have you done now?" asked Billy as he held up the New York Daily News, a gossipy tabloid. The front page had a huge photograph of the late Brenda Barratt with a blaring headline in the boldest of fonts, all caps.

PLAZA MURDER!
FAMED AUTHOR QUESTIONED!

Devon gawked at it.

All he could say was "Oh, fuck!"

Billy Bennett and Peyton Chase had returned home from London less than six months earlier after helping Devon Stone eliminate a few devious Nazi sympathizers. Devon had done more than simply "write murders". Both Billy and Peyton, friends since childhood, served as army pilots during World War II. They both had been severely wounded and both had been awarded the Purple Heart medal.

5

The Dover Preservation Society was located in a converted, well-kept Victorian-era house on Prospect Street, a few short blocks from the town's center. The walls in the small entryway were lined with old photographs of Dover's history. Photos of businesses, large and small homes, people, and pets of all kind graced the collection. The parlor to the right of the front door had been converted into an office whose walls were also filled with framed pieces. There were several pieces of original artwork interspersed amongst the photographs. The collection included oil paintings of various sizes, with watercolors, etchings and drawings preserved behind glass and ornate frames. Shelves in the larger room, the living room, were lined with books and ledgers filled with bits of history left behind by generations, including births, deaths, weddings, and funerals dating back to the early 1800s. Visitors who stepped over the front porch threshold through the heavy wooden front door were greeted with the musty aroma of the past and a nearby train whistle broke the silence several times a day. The Delaware, Lackawanna and Western Railroad had built the old red brick station, just a few blocks away from the Preservation Society, in 1901. Another part of Dover's old history.

It was usually more quiet within its walls than the local library, and visited with even less frequency. But not this morning. Shortly after she arrived to open the door at 10 A.M. and before she could even switch on the lights, Allyson Langston, the society's attractive young director, heard the telephone ringing. An unusual occurrence on most days but it wouldn't be today. She hastily put her purse down on her desk and reached for the phone.

"Good morning," she answered cheerfully, "Preservation Society, this is Ally Langston. May I help you?"

She listened as the caller stated the reason for the early morning call. She gasped, bringing one hand up to her mouth, nearly dropping the receiver.

"Oh, my god, that's horrible," she said, now nearly in tears. "I can't believe that. I simply cannot believe that. That poor woman. Oh, my god."

She listened further.

"No. No, I haven't heard anything about it, Alice. I didn't have the radio on this morning and I don't have a television. I don't imagine it was in the papers yet." She listened some more. "What? Oh, of course the Daily News *would*, wouldn't you know it?"

The caller spoke for a few more minutes, and Allyson Langston listened intently.

"Thank you for letting me know about this awful situation. This horrifies me, as you can imagine. This has totally ruined my day. Oh, that sounds so callous, now, doesn't it? I'm sorry."

And she ended the call.

She sat down at her desk, leaning back into the old leather swivel chair and wiped a few tears from her face that had trickled down her cheeks. She looked around settling her gaze upon a particular old oil painting that was hanging in the hallway directly across from her open office doorway. She stared up at it. She hated the ominous painting. She hated it even more now, following the news about Brenda Barratt. It frightened her. Most visitors to the facility scurried past it, hardly giving it a glace. It was *that* hideous. Rarely, in all the past years, had anyone questioned its purpose or its history. Nor did anyone pay any attention to the tiny dedication plaque beneath it.

But that was about to change.

A sudden shrill train whistle startled her and she jumped. Picking up a pen, she nervously fidgeted with it, tapping it on her desk. She sighed deeply, dropped the pen and began drumming her fingers. She stopped that and reached for her telephone once again. She dialed and waited. After six rings the phone was answered.

"Jeff, it's me," she said. "What? Yes, I just now heard. Weren't you going to call me? This certainly changes the whole scenario now, doesn't it? Should we be worried? Are *we* in any possible danger?"

20

Allyson Langston listened as her brother, Jefferson, a lawyer, spoke. A look of concern crept across her face as he confirmed what she already knew. That he had planned to meet with Brenda Barratt within the next few days.

6

"You certainly have a unique approach to doing research for your books, Devon," laughed Peyton Chase as both he and Billy stepped into the hotel room.

"Oh, blast," replied Devon, shaking their hands with a warm greeting and closing the door behind them. "Who would have expected that such a short chance meeting would end up as headlines, eh? I feel so sorry for that poor woman."

"I don't know how you feel about such things," Billy said, "but, personally, I don't believe there is any such thing as a coincidence. You were meant to meet her, even if your association was brief."

"Rubbish," huffed Devon Stone.

"I thought you were supposed to *write* murders, not *commit* them. Oh, wait. Never mind!" Peyton couldn't control his laughter this time.

"In the short time that I've known you, Mr. Chase," said Devon with a mocking smile, "I have observed that you speak fluent sarcasm."

"I just may consider teaching it as a second language at the local college," Peyton laughed, returning Devon's mocking smile.

"Getting off the subject of murder for a moment," Devon Stone said looking back and forth from one man to the other, "have your female companions joined you here back in the States?"

Billy Bennett's girlfriend was the popular American actress and singer, Veronica Barron. She had been living and performing in London following World War II. She and Billy had met while he, as an army pilot, was stationed in Europe and she performed in a touring USO group. Peyton Chase had been smitten with a young Russian woman who had been helping Devon Stone with the assassins targeting the heroines, the Night Witches, who had bombed Nazi targets in the Soviet Union. Initially known to Billy, Veronica, and Peyton as Alexis Morgan, her true identity of Anoushka Markarova was revealed as the deadly plot played out. A spark had ignited between Peyton and Anoushka and it grew into a flame.

"Anoushka was here visiting with me for a couple months," answered Peyton. "We had a great time and I honestly think we can make things work. She had to return home to attend to some family matters and, frankly, to work out a sticky situation with a passport or two. She'll be back as soon as possible, though! I hope."

"Ronnie is finishing up her run in *Private Lives* within the month," Billy interjected. "She is really eager, now, to get back to the States and take Broadway by storm. She was here briefly and actually auditioned a couple months ago for the second lead role in an upcoming show called *Can-Can*. Why she tried out for something other than the lead was beyond me, but I guess she's just eager to get on a Broadway stage. Anyway, the writers and choreographer wanted someone younger. Younger than the ripe old age of thirty-three, evidently. So a basically unknown dancer beat her out. I think the ingénue's name was a Gwen somebody or other…uh, Gwen Verdon, or something like that. In any event, she'll be heading back to the good old U.S. of A. permanently within the next couple of weeks."

Devon Stone tensed up as the telephone rang yet again.

"I just may pull that bloody thing out of the wall!" he said tersely. "That had damn well be either my American publisher calling or Alfred Hitchcock with a sizeable film offer!"

It was neither.

"Good afternoon again, Mr. Stone," said the apparently ever-cheerful receptionist at the front desk. "I so sincerely apologize for an oversight on the hotel's behalf. A courier delivered an envelope for you early last evening. Things became terribly hectic down here with a huge rush of late check-ins and that envelope must have gotten lost in the shuffle. I shall send a bellhop with it up to your room immediately. Please, accept our sincerest apologies and I hope it wasn't something that you had been expecting last night." And she clicked off. He explained the call to his two friends.

"Well," sighed Devon, "I wasn't expecting anything but maybe my publisher was sending over some information before we had our face-to-face."

A knock came and Devon opened the door while reaching into his wallet to give the bellhop a dollar. The tip was accepted with a smile and a short bow before Devon once again closed the door.

He examined the envelope with his name and The Algonquin Hotel written in beautiful cursive. It was on the Plaza Hotel stationery. He arched his eyebrows as he carefully tore open the back flap on the envelope and extracted a letter. Billy and Peyton looked back and forth at each other as Devon slowly read the enclosure written in that same beautiful cursive, his eyes widening and letting out a soft, low groan. He slowly sank into the nearest chair, letting the letter slip from his hands and fall onto the floor.

"Bloody hell," he exclaimed softly. "This puts a whole new wrinkle in the fabric. Bloody, bloody hell!"

7

Billy leaned over and picked up the letter that Devon had dropped. Peyton looked over his shoulder as they both started to read it.

Dear Mr. Stone,

I had first considered calling you at the Algonquin but thought better of it. I didn't want to intrude upon any plans you may have had for this evening after our long flight. Apologies for falling asleep on the plane. I did want to discuss something with you after my pleasant surprise of finding you to be a fellow passenger. Serendipity I suppose.

Not to bore you with my life story, but I am returning home to a rather contentious situation. One of which I've been trying to avoid. But time is running out. Not trying to be overly melodramatic, but I have actually received a couple thinly veiled threats. Hopefully the situation may be resolved peacefully within the week.

Here I come being brazen again. I hope that we may be able to get together, or at least converse on the telephone before you return home to London. Maybe you'll be on a book tour and you can come to New Jersey. I'm not sure. But, with this situation I'm facing, there could be a frightening and intriguing plot at hand for one of your future books. I'm serious, Mr. Stone. I'm not just some old crazy biddy prattling nonsense.

Until we meet again...

Sincerely,
B.B.

"Whoa," whispered Billy as he and Peyton stared at a now-despondent Devon Stone.

"For Pete's sake, Devon," Peyton said, "I don't know what the implications were in that note...I mean about her situation...but it doesn't involve you and you couldn't have prevented the outcome."

"I realize that," answered Devon, now standing up and pacing around the room. "But if she had received threats, mild or otherwise, I would have hoped that she had contacted the authorities of some kind. Of course, now there's no way of knowing that."

"I'm curious," interjected Billy, "about her contentious situation, whatever it might have been. But, as you just said, there's no way of knowing about it now."

"You've missed out, evidently," voiced Peyton, "on a potential book plot. I didn't mean for that to sound as callous as it did."

Devon Stone just stared at him for a moment, shaking his head.

"Well, this note might be a piece of evidence I suppose," Devon said after a moment of silence. "But for whom and for what? It's lacking details aside from the part about threats but, actually, that too is meaningless now. And what did she mean by time is running out? I honestly don't know what I should do now. I'm flummoxed."

"We have two other people to contend with," Jefferson Langston said into the phone, "one of whom appears to be missing and has been for years. For all we know, he might even be dead. This may not end as well or as easily as we had hoped."

"But what do we do now?" asked Allyson.

"I haven't a clue," answered her brother, "but at least this gives us a bit more time. The plot thickens, as they say in all those crappy old murder mysteries."

8

Devon Stone was a pen name. The name that appeared on his passport, Daniel Stein (Stein being German for stone), was known only to a select few. He was now regretting using his pen name to make his hotel reservations, and made a mental note to remedy that situation in the future.

Because of all the commotion following the headlines blaring in the boldest of fonts about the *PLAZA MURDER*, Devon Stone pushed back his meeting with his American publisher by one day. He was more than grateful for that. Not for the murder, but for the time to decompress at his hotel. But he couldn't get Brenda Barratt's note to him out of his mind. More specifically, out of his vivid imagination. He remained in his suite and tried to relax for the remainder of that first day. As much as a mystery writer *can* relax, especially with his name being bandied about in the media. Room service supplied all three of his meals, which he regretted to a degree. Although the food was actually quite good, there were so many fine restaurants around the area, but he really didn't want to venture out. Although he was sure they had all departed and had forgotten about him, Devon Stone was wary about members of the press lying in wait if he should make an appearance. By evening, the large bottle of Gordon's Gin was empty. He finally drifted off to a restless sleep around midnight.

He awoke, completely refreshed, practically at dawn and prepared for his meeting. He took his time...the meeting wasn't until 11:30. He scribbled some last-minute thoughts he had about the book he was currently writing, packing them into his attaché case. He hoped that he could avoid any discussion of the *current* murder situation while he was with his publisher.

Freshly bathed and dressed in his most dapper suit and tie, he enjoyed a quick coffee and cheese Danish before walking through the hotel lobby and the awaiting car-horn honking hubbub of Manhattan. He placed his stylish Trilby hat upon his head, tipping it as he winked at the pretty young clerk at the reception desk as he headed out to begin his day. He wondered if she had been the one to tip off the lurking media the morning after the horrendous murder.

"Cab, sir?" asked the very formal doorman when he exited the hotel door.

Devon Stone inhaled, looked up at the crisp, clear blue sky and declined the offer.

"Thanks, chap," he said to the doorman. "But, no. It looks like a perfectly nice day for walking and I really don't have that far to go."

"Very well, sir," replied the doorman with a slight salute as he stepped back into his post. "Enjoy your walk."

Devon was not unfamiliar with this city. He enjoyed the hustle and haste of the New Yorkers. They were always in a hurry to get somewhere, even if they really had nowhere in particular to go. Even their speech patterns were fast and clipped. He inhaled deeply through his nose once again. Manhattan had a distinct aroma. Automobile and bus exhaust, combined with scents from street vendors, steaming vents, and teeming humanity. Seeing no obvious members of the press lurking around, he stepped down from the hotel and turned east, toward Fifth Avenue. He stopped on the corner for a moment. A few blocks to the north would be the beautiful Scribner's Bookstore. *I'll stop in there later*, he thought to himself, *to see how many of mine they have on display.* He turned, then, to the south. He saw his destination waiting for him in the distance: the Empire State Building.

He picked up his pace to match his fellow pedestrians, but stopped when he came to the front of the New York Public Library. He stood and admired the massive stone lions guarding the wide stairway leading up to the building entrance. Topped by a large blue and yellow umbrella with the word *SABRETT* in all caps, a wheeled hot dog cart off to the right of the staircase seemed to be doing a brisk, early lunchtime business. Fifteen cents for a frankfurter in a bun with onions and mustard. Five cents more would get a soda of his choosing. Devon could smell the aroma and was momentarily tempted to join the line waiting, but he knew that a two-martini business luncheon would soon take place a few blocks further south. In his particular case, it would probably be a two-gin & tonic luncheon. Or more.

He reached his destination and looked upward. The design and construction of this landmark, the tallest building in the world, was such that it appeared to taper toward the top. He entered the expansive lobby, awash with shiny, reflective marble and headed straight for the bank of elevators. He was always impressed by the towering aluminum relief artwork depicting the building itself in adoring art deco style at the back wall. He stood and waited for the elevator that would take him up to the thirty-seventh floor. The light above the elevator doors flashed on and a soft ding announced the car's arrival. He waited while the passengers got out before entering it.

Devon Stone glanced at the nametag worn by the uniformed elevator operator as he entered the car.

"Thirty-seven, please. And is your name *really* Otis, young man?" he asked.

The elevator operator, who was sixty-years-old if he was a day, rolled his eyes.

"Yes, sir, it is," the old man replied politely but halfheartedly. Obviously not the first time he had heard this. Nor would it be the last. Sheer coincidence notwithstanding. He waited for the inevitable trite joke.

"I'll just go ahead and assume that your last name *isn't* Elevator, then." Devon said with a wink.

A few of his fellow passengers snickered. No reaction from Otis.

The elevator slowly climbed upwards, with a few stops on various floors.

The elevator operator turned and smiled at Devon. "I have been an elevator operator here ever since this magnificent piece of architecture first opened in 1931. You might want to ask me if I enjoy my job, sir. Many people do and seem to enjoy my response."

"*Do* you enjoy your job? And your response would be…?" asked Devon.

"It has its ups and downs," answered Otis, shrugging his shoulders and adding a big wink.

Now it was Devon's turn to roll his eyes.

"Here we are, sir. Thirty-seven. Watch your step and have a good day."

Upon exiting the elevator, he turned toward the double glass doors with the large, impressive Bruin Publishing Company logo etched into each one.

The attractive redheaded receptionist smiled broadly when she saw Devon Stone enter. Women always seemed to react this way to this handsome man and they flirted shamelessly.

"Good morning, Mr. Stone," she said with a lilting voice, almost purring. "Welcome back. It's always a pleasure to have you in our offices. I shall alert the powers that be of your arrival."

Devon wasn't sure but he thought she winked at him. "Thank you, Valencia," he said, smiling back at her.

"Oh, I'm so impressed that you remember my name, Mr. Stone. We met only briefly the last time you were here a couple of years ago."

Devon chuckled.

"You'd be surprised, my dear, what I remember."

She made a quick phone call and five minutes later Devon heard a booming voice coming down the hall into the lobby.

"Devon, Devon, Devon," said Bankston Bruin as he outstretched his hand. "Man, it's so great seeing you again!"

Bankston Bruin, Marketing Director and Chief Editor for the Bruin Publishing Company (his father's company), was in his early 60s, balding, perhaps twenty pounds overweight, and just as dapper as Devon regarding attire.

"I hope you weren't waiting here in the lobby too long. I was finishing a long call and my girl just informed me that you had arrived."

"No, no. No problem, Banks," responded Devon Stone. "I was just waiting over there by the windows in case I saw King Kong fall."

Bankston Bruin laughed.

"You know, I was told that tourism to this building increased after that silly movie came out years ago. I'm surprised that they aren't selling little stuffed toy gorillas in the lobby gift shop. Curiosity and human nature, right? That's what sells. More specifically, that's what sells murder mysteries."

"This is my favorite building here in Manhattan," said Devon as he glanced out the windows once again. "Well, it's a tossup between this and that gorgeous Chrysler Building. Did you know that *this* building, from start to finish, was completed in just eighteen months? From start to finish! Amazing."

"Mmm, no," said Bankston Bruin shaking his head and shrugging his shoulders, not knowing what else to say or do. "I didn't know that. How did *you* know that?"

Devon Stone laughed. "I'm a writer, and I know things."

"Well, then, Mr. Writer, come on back to the conference room. We'll head out to luncheon very soon. I'm sure you must be hungry. Or thirsty. Have I got an interesting tidbit to tell you! Can I have my girl get you some coffee or something?"

"No, thanks," answered Devon. "I'm fine. And I'm eager to hear what you have to say. And also eager to move past the events of the past day or so."

"Well, my friend, just *wait* until you hear what I'm about to tell you. This can play out in our respective favors."

Devon Stone followed Bankston down a long hallway lined with framed book covers from countless dozens of murder mysteries, Devon's included. They entered an expansive conference room and Bankston flicked on the lights. Propped up on six easels were enlargements of book cover prototypes for the book of Devon's they were about to publish in the States, *Beacon of Betrayal*. Devon's eyes widened when he saw them.

"Sit, sit, sit, Devon," said Bruin, "We'll get to those mock-ups very shortly. I have some rather urgent news to impart."

The two men seated themselves across from each other on the polished oak conference table. There were notepads with pencils and pens beside them. Devon knew that at some time during the day a lawyer or two would join them. The plush chairs were comfortable and Devon almost sighed as he sank back into one of them.

"Let me say right off that it's an absolute delight to have you back in the States, Devon. We have been so proud to have you as one of our most popular authors. That's about to change."

"Uh, oh," said Devon with trepidation. "Why do I have the feeling that you are about to hit me with some unsettling news?"

Bankston Bruin smiled, leaned forward and steepled his fingers.

"Ever since the news broke yesterday morning and especially with your name attached to it, our switchboard has been going crazy."

"And that's a bad thing, right?" asked Devon, wrinkling his brow.

"Jesus, man, on the contrary. On the contrary! Remember what I said a few minutes ago out in the lobby about human nature and curiosity? This Barratt murder is a bonanza, for chrissake! Our pre-publication orders are now skyrocketing. Doubling as we now speak. Bookstores on the proposed list for the tour are doubling. They want you, man. They want you badly. You have just become our number *one* most popular author!"

Devon leaned further back in the chair, sinking into the comfort and simply shook his head. He was not going to relate to Bankston Bruin the note that the poor murdered woman had written to him, probably no more than an hour or so before her brutal slaying. He even debated whether or not to reveal that note to Detective Lafferty. A decision he would make before returning to his hotel room.

"But, Banks, I had absolutely *nothing* to do with the murder. I spoke to the poor woman for…hmm…fifteen minutes tops. If that!"

"No matter, Devon. Doesn't matter at all. Ever since we first heard about the murder yesterday morning, our legal department and our research department have been working furiously. We uncovered some tidbits that you, as an esteemed murder aficionado, might be intrigued by. Oooohhh, I see a future book, Devon Stone, and it would blow the roof off of sales. A great plot if ever there was one!"

I have more plots than I can handle at the moment, thought Devon Stone, inwardly shaking his head.

Bankston Bruin stood up and reached for the telephone. "Belinda," he said when his secretary answered, "Please have Tony join us in the conference room. Thanks, dear, and please hold all my calls. I'm sure we'll be heading out to lunch soon. We're ravenous in here!"

He hung up the phone and returned his attention to Devon.

"I'm having Tony Dunlap join us, Devon. He's the art director responsible for these design concepts here. But there is another reason I want him in here. You're not going to believe this. He has a very strange, coincidental connection to the murder victim, Brenda Barratt."

Devon Stone looked askance.

At 11:30, Billy Bennett reached for the door to their gun shop and hung the sign *OUT TO LUNCH – Will Return at* and he changed the moveable hands on the printed clock face on the sign to read *12:30*. He closed and locked the door with Peyton Chase waiting for him on the sidewalk. Their popular gun shop was located on a side street a few steps from Blackwell Street, the main street through Dover. They walked just a few steps further up the block to Sallie's Bella Luna Trattoria, their favorite little casual restaurant. Salvatore Bertolli, known to all his friends and customers as Sallie, poked his head out from the kitchen and greeted them when they entered. *I Get A Kick Out Of You* sung by Frank Sinatra was playing on the jukebox.

"Hey, you bums back again?" he shouted. "Tryin' to beat the lunchtime crowd or are ya hiding out from the cops?"

"Ha!" shouted Peyton right back at him. "We're trying to beat the Health Department here, before they close you down. They're in the next block and heading this way."

Sallie laughed and clapped his hands together, shaking his head.

"Don't bust my chops, flyboy," he called out with a wave of his hand. "I'll be sure to sprinkle some extra arsenic along with the Parmigiano in your dish today."

They all laughed as the two friends headed toward their favorite table by the window. They didn't need a menu. They knew it by heart.

"The usual, boys?" asked Stella, Sallie's wife of nearly twenty years.

"Yeah, but let's switch it up a bit today, Stella," answered Peyton with a sly grin. "Give me his," indicating Billy, "and give him mine."

"Funny. Very funny. I'll try not to mix it up when I bring them out," Stella answered.

Each man, with rare exception, almost always ordered the Eggplant Parmesan, Linguini Pomodoro, with a side salad.

Billy had picked up a copy of the Dover Advance, the local newspaper, from the stand out in front of the restaurant. No surprise to either of them, but the headlines still blared about the murder of an elderly Morristown woman while in New York City. Billy took a sip from the glass of Coca-Cola that Stella had delivered and scanned through the story about Brenda Barratt. He hesitated when he hit a particular sentence regarding the Dover Preservation Society.

"Hmm. Interesting," he said, causing Peyton to look up. "What were those two words that Devon told us were on that note found in the murdered lady's room, can you remember?"

Peyton thought for a second, scrunching up his face.

"Latin. Something in Latin, right? Memento something or other, I think."

"Could it be *this*?" Billy said as he held up the newspaper.

"Well, I'll be damned!" exclaimed Peyton as he saw the photograph and read the caption. "This certainly *does* put another wrinkle in the fabric!"

Allyson Langston was not usually the nervous type, but today she was on edge. Fidgety. The events of the past few days unnerved her in more ways than one. She knew the situation was going to be a messy, unpleasant one but she never figured that murder would be in the mix. She got up from her old wooden desk and slowly paced around her office. She went to the window and looked out onto tree-lined Prospect Street with other beautiful Victorian-era houses on both sides. Some had been renovated to their past glory. Some had not. She smiled as she watched a dog as it tried to chase a squirrel up a tall, old oak tree in the front yard of the house next door. The shrill whistle from a train as it pulled away from the station a few blocks away broke the silence and made her jump. It was a sunny morning, filling her office with brilliant springtime light, with the slats from the old wooden Venetian blinds casting striped shadows across her face as she stood there. She saw that a few puffy clouds were beginning to float above in the sky. She sat back down in her leather chair as she heard the front door to the building open. No one had come into the house for days, but that was not unusual. People looking up their family history, browsing through old journals or, sometimes, students doing research papers for school visited the facility sporadically. It might be weeks between anyone coming in. She thought about heading out for lunch when the person had finished and left. She listened to the measured footsteps as whoever it was moved slowly through the rooms. She could hear as the footsteps crossed the hardwood floors, then the footfalls sounded more softly as whoever it was walked across the few scattered rugs that were throughout the house.

The sound of walking suddenly stopped. She was about to reach for the phone to call her brother once again when the person slowly pushed open the partially closed door to her office and entered the room. A cloud obscured the sun at that moment, darkening her office. She looked up and smiled.

"Good morning," she said, "How may I help you?"

The response was a bullet as it shot straight through the center of her forehead. She slammed back into her now-blood splattered chair and then slowly slid off onto the floor.

9

Six thousand, two hundred and eighty-five miles away as the crow flies, Alistair Stickle awoke with a hangover and smelling of rum. He yawned, stretched and looked out of his large, open bedroom window. A brilliant early autumn sun was slowly making its way above the horizon, casting blinding, sparkling rays of light like a thousand golden coins skittering across the southern Pacific waters. He heard his normal wakeup call, the deep hooting coos of a Dark-backed Imperial Pigeon perched in a tree along side of his small cottage. Regular as clockwork, the bird was there every morning at dawn.

He sat up, swung his long legs around planting his feet on the floor, waiting for a few moments to allow his head to stop spinning.

"Good morning, Samantha," he called out to the bird. He used a different name just about every morning. The bird responded with its greeting *whuup...whuup...*and Alistair Stickle laughed. He chuckled to himself as he watched a small gecko scamper up the wall heading toward the open window, stopping to turn and look at him before jumping to the ground below.

He finally stood up and strolled, naked, out of his small hut, walking through the palm trees and down to the water's edge. At 29, and in great physical shape, his lithe tanned body moved with grace. The strong tropical sun had bleached his naturally blond hair, even making the hair on his chest and muscular legs stand out more. He had no neighbors, having selected his living quarters in a remote section of the island on purpose. The sandy beach slanted easily into the beautiful crystal clear turquoise water and Alistair walked in casually, before diving under the water when it reached thigh-high. Coming up quickly, he broke the water's surface, shaking the water from his head and took several strokes further out. He rolled over onto his back, floating straight out, letting the warmth of the rising sun caress the entire front of his body. He watched as a few Tahiti petrels swooped overhead in the cloudless azure sky, calling with their nasal shrieks and whistles.

Seeing a small single-outrigger canoe approaching from the south, Alistair Stickle rolled back over, concealing his nakedness as much as possible beneath the clear water.

Two small children he recognized as distant neighbors called out to him with a singsong accent.

"Oh, bon jour, monsieur Tuttle!" one of them called, waving a small brown hand. "*Maita'i oe,* monsieur Tuttle?" called the second child.

"*Maita'i roa, maururu.* I am fine, thanks," Alistair answered back, also waving his hand.

And they paddled off again, perhaps back to their home.

No one on this island knew his real name.

~

The editor glanced at his watch.

"Good! Almost time for lunch. I can't remember if I've ever taken you to Major's Cabin when you've been here in the past, Devon," said Bankston Bruin. "I'm a fairly regular customer and Major Satz and I are pretty chummy. The restaurant is only a few steps away from this building so it's nice and convenient. They have the best prime rib and chops around. Hey, I know you like trivia and you seem to remember all that kinda stuff. You know, facts and figures…and dates. I'll bet you didn't know that the very first Diners Club credit card was used at Majors Cabin, did you? File *that* away in your vast memory bank, Devon. Wait until we have a short chat with Tony and we'll head out, okay?"

Devon Stone smiled and nodded, "You're hosting this party, Banks. Whatever you say is fine with me." *Prime rib?* Devon totally discarded the thought about the hot dog cart he had seen on his walk here earlier.

A few minutes later there was a soft knocking on the conference room door.

"Come on in, Tony," called Bankston. "We're waiting for ya!"

The door opened and Tony Dunlap stepped quietly into the room.

Dark-haired and in his early-thirties, Tony Dunlap had been the senior art director at Bruin Publishing since returning from serving during World

War Two. He was highly respected, greatly talented, and had won several prestigious awards from the Art Directors Club of New York.

"Sorry I won't be able to join you for lunch, guys," he said, "but sometimes deadlines and last minute changes take precedence, ya know?"

"Oh, bloody hell," laughed Devon, "Don't I know it!"

"Sit, sit, sit. Okay, then," said Bankston as he rubbed his hands together. "Before we go to lunch and really get down to the business of books, Tony, please tell Devon your unbelievable connection to that murdered lady."

"Well, honestly I don't have a connection to *her*, per se. I never met Brenda Barratt. I only knew *about* her. And I was told some intriguing stories by her grandson. We both served together in the army during World War Two and were part of a highly classified mission."

"This is the part that would make a *great* book for you, Devon!" exclaimed Bankston Bruin.

"Not sure if you should, not *yet* anyway, Devon," responded Tony Dunlap. "It's still classified and I'm not sure when or if the public will ever find out about it. Anyway, to cut to the chase, I was a good friend with Miss Barratt's grandson. As I just mentioned, we served, side by side, in our mission. Soon after our discharge, he vanished. He's been missing for seven years. I'm pretty sure I know why. But I have no idea where he might be, or if he is even still alive. I've not forgotten him. His name is Stickle. Alistair Stickle."

Alistair Stickle, Ben Tuttle to those who knew him on the island of Mo'orea, took several more long strokes in the crystal clear waters, making the colorful fishes beneath him dart in various directions. Perfectly at ease with his nakedness in the open air, he ambled back off the beach and into his cottage. He called it a hut because of its steep pitched thatched roof. Having lived in this little abode for almost eighteen months, this was the longest he had stayed in one place, in any country for the past seven years. He had an outdoor shower installed with a concrete slab just at the rear entryway and he washed off the sand and salt water before heading to his tiny kitchen to brew his first pot of coffee for the day.

Quite often he would remain naked and alone for days on end. But today would be different. As his coffee brewed he took a real shower with soap and hot water in his cramped bathroom. He shaved off five days' worth of stubbly beard and, owning no underwear at all, pulled on a pair of clean khaki shorts and buttoned up (halfway) a weathered khaki shirt. He tied a bright red bandana around his now clean-shaven neck. He glanced into the mirror and winked at himself. His reflection winked back.

Freshly brewed and steaming coffee in hand, he went into the largest room in the small abode. It would usually be, for normal people, a living room. But this was his studio. A large easel stood erect nearest a large open window. Canvasses of various sizes were stacked, back-to-back against two of the walls. Cabinets and tables overflowed with dozens of tubes of oil paints. Cans of turpentine were tucked under one of the tables. Brushes of all sizes protruded from now-empty coffee tins. He had already selected six canvasses, each a painting in brilliant colors depicting both landscapes and animals indigenous to the island. On occasion he would paint beautiful native women. Many of them nudes. His paintings usually sold very quickly to the few rich tourists who often stopped at this island as they cruised the South Pacific. There was no airport on Tahiti so tourism was relegated to the snobby rich with large enough windjammers or yachts that sailed from island to island, usually beginning and ending in Australia. Several of his paintings, however, lined the walls of the wealthy pineapple plantation owners on the island. His largest painting done while on the island hangs in the office of the most prominent Tahitian Black Pearl Farm. To his chagrin, the most popular subject matter for the tourists, and the one he paints often because it never fails to sell, was of a large yellow lizard. The Tahitian word *Mo'ore'a* means "yellow lizard". And it's the legend of how the island got its name that makes the gullible tourists buy *anything* involving lizards from the few tacky souvenir shops that were on Tahiti, a ferryboat ride from where Alistair Stickle stood.

Air Tahiti had been formed three short years earlier and operated only between Pape'ete, the capital city of French Polynesia, Raiatea, the second largest of the islands, and Bora Bora. No airport was needed, as the only aircraft utilized was a Grumman Widgeon J-4F, a 7-seater seaplane. In 1951 it inaugurated fortnightly mail service between Pape'ete and the Cook Islands.

Alistair Stickle tied the selected canvasses together with heavy twine and loaded them into the back of his dusty old Jeep. Driving toward the harbor, he saw the ferry from Pape'ete as it was approaching the dock. He had timed it just right. The ferry would unload what few passengers it carried, some fresh produce from local markets and perhaps some mail and newspapers that had been delivered via the seaplane earlier that morning. One hour later the ferry would head back to Pape'ete and Alistair would be aboard. He waited patiently on the dock until it was time to board. He did so, carrying his canvasses and a cold bottle of soda he had gotten from a stand nearby. He went to his favorite spot on the very top deck so he could watch the beautiful island as the boat departed. He leaned his wrapped paintings against a wooden bench as he deeply inhaled the always-refreshing aroma of the sea. A gentle zephyr ruffled his hair, the ferry captain blew the horn announcing the departure and they were heading out into the sound between Tahiti and the sister island of Mo'ore'a. The intense, deep blue color of the water between the islands reminded Alistair Stickle of the colors of the Aegean.

Less than an hour later, he was walking down the main street in Pape'ete heading toward the small gallery where his paintings would be displayed and, hopefully, be sold. It was called the Yellow Lizard Galerie d'Arte, and a modest in size but well-appointed flat above the gallery was home to its owner.

"Well, well, well," called out Martine Blanc, the voluptuous, fetchingly beautiful owner of the gallery as she saw Alistair enter. "Welcome back, my handsome young Gauguin," she laughed, as Alistair coyly shook his head. "It has been a couple weeks, so I was expecting you any day now with some new paintings for me."

No more than a year older than Alistair, Martine spoke with a lilting accent, had long ebony hair that draped over shapely, tanned shoulders. Her dark, almond-shaped eyes sparkled. She had a trim waist and wore a flimsy, filmy pale blue blouse, provocatively unbuttoned halfway. The blouse was worn, untucked, over a pair of white wide-legged trousers. He kissed her on both cheeks and she returned the favor. They stared into each other's eyes for a brief moment. And, looking around to be sure they were alone, they fell into a passionate kiss. She smelled of jasmine; he smelled of Lifebuoy soap. He reached under and up into her blouse gently massaging a supple breast as she reached down placing her hand on his now erect crotch. They pulled back from each other quickly as someone passed by the open doorway.

"Business first," snickered Martine as she winked at him. "Before pleasure. I'm sure pleasure will tire us both out for the rest of the day."

It usually did.

Although it was just a couple days old, a newspaper from the United States lay crumpled up on a stool next to the cash register. Martine used old newspapers for wrapping and packing paintings and the other object's d'art she sold. She would use the local newspaper or, if tourists happened to be reading news from overseas, she would ask them not to discard it and give it to her. Alistair never paid any attention to the news, no matter *where* it came from. Never listened to the radio, and television was too rare on these islands. He was oblivious to the world other than the tropics. He just happened to glance down at this particular newspaper and he gasped. He picked it up and read it. His heart stopped and he froze. His future had just been rear-ended by his past.

There would be no pleasure this afternoon.

10

"We were ghosts during the war," said Tony Dunlap, "in that secret mission."

"Excuse me?" questioned Devon, thinking perhaps he had misinterpreted. "I'm not sure I heard you correctly."

"I'll explain, Devon, but until I know for sure the story is cleared for public knowledge, please, I implore you, do *not* write about it or tell anyone else about it."

"Are you sure you can even tell *me?*" asked Devon, a bit concerned. "Although you've obviously spilled some of the beans, so to speak, to Bankston here."

"It will explain my odd connection to the current murder mystery that occurred at the Plaza a couple nights ago. It might lead to my locating my long-missing army buddy. Assuming, that is, he is still among the living."

Bankston leaned back in his chair, folding his hands on the conference room table and nodded to Tony to continue.

"Okay," began Tony slowly. "This secret mission sounds like something straight out of the movies. Perhaps the Keystone Cops or even Laurel and Hardy. I just said that we were ghosts during the war. In actuality we were part of the secret mission called the Ghost Army, although we were officially known as the 23rd Headquarters Special Troops. Alistair, Al to me, and I were two of an eleven hundred-man unit. Our mission was to impersonate other, much larger Allied Army units to deceive the enemy."

"And exactly *how* were you to do that little trick?" asked Devon, still unbelieving but highly interested.

"With balloons," laughed Bankston Bruin. Tony Dunlap shot him a look.

"No. Not quite balloons," continued Tony, shaking his head. "But… okay, don't laugh…we created large, life-size inflatable vehicles. Trucks.

Jeeps. Tanks. Even cannons and aircraft. All looking like the real thing from the air."

Devon Stone sat way back into his comfortable chair and stared intently at Tony.

"Why do I have the feeling, Tony," Devon said, narrowing his eyes and increasing the intensity of his stare, "that you are making this up. This must be some kind of ruse to see how gullible I really am, right?"

Tony Dunlap held up his right hand, "Honest injun, Devon. Scout's honor and all that stuff. This is true. We, also, thought it was too bizarre when we were first recruited for the mission. Thought we'd be sitting ducks and vanquished the first day."

Devon continued the stare but sat forward, now, in his chair.

"Go on," he said. "Then this situation isn't going where I thought it was. You have me hooked, young man. Continue."

Billy Bennett tried to reach Devon Stone at the Algonquin on the telephone but was told that the author had left the hotel earlier in the day. He hadn't checked out yet, though, as his reservation was for at least four more days.

"Wanna head into the city with me buddy?" he asked Peyton. "No doubt Devon will really need to see *this*," as he held up the newspaper they had read at lunchtime.

"Sure, why not?" Peyton Chase answered. "If for no other reason you can entice me with a nice hot pastrami on rye at Katz's."

"Hmm," chuckled Billy, using his hands like a scale, weighing the options. "Let's see. Murder? Pastrami? Tough call, there, buddy."

"I'm not kidding, Devon," continued Tony Dunlap. "We were skeptical but evidently the stupid Nazis believed that we were a huge, dangerous unit. Actually, we were the first mobile, tactical deception unit in U.S. Army history. *Now* I'm proud to say that. We were able to convince those idiots that we were two whole divisions…you know, approximately 30,000 strong. We used visual, sonic, and radio deception. Believe it or not, all of us were carefully chosen. Most of us were graphic designers, artists, actors, sound effects engineers, and photographers. Many of us "ghosts" were recruits from art schools in New York and Philly. We all played our roles very well, I must say. We "staged" phony radio traffic, using special sound effects. To top it all off, we were armed with nothing heavier than .50 caliber machine guns! And, yes, our inflatable vehicles looked remarkably realistic from the air. Sometimes we didn't completely camouflage the vehicles, on purpose of course, so the stupid Krauts could see them and, needless to say, misidentify them."

Devon continued to stare, almost not believing what he was being told.

"Al...I mean Alistair Stickle and I were both designers. He is...or was...about a year or two younger than me. I was a young assistant art director at BBD&O when I enlisted in the army. Ironically, one of the agency's founders, Alex Osborn coined the term and technique called "brainstorming" to generate ideas. That sure came in handy when I became a ghost! As far as Al was concerned, he was trying to make a go as a fine artist before enlisting. That certainly came in handy as well."

"Okay, then," interrupted Devon, "but you said he disappeared after the war. Mysteriously, I take it. And does his disappearance have anything to do with his murdered grandmother?"

Devon Stone was interested in this story but he was getting frustrated. He was here in the United States to conduct book business, not become part of another crime scene. He was torn. And he was eager for Tony to get to the end of his story. But Devon sensed that Tony was far from the end at this point.

"Well, yes and no," answered Tony. "Al was extremely close to his grandmother. She was very much into the arts and supported his desire to go into design or painting. From what he told me, she must have been a lot younger than most of the other kids' grandmothers. She would take him into the city to museums, art galleries, and Broadway shows when he was growing up. He really never mentioned his parents that much. I had a feeling that some friction existed but I never found out exactly why. A few nights following our discharge from the army we were both out drinking with a couple of our other army buddies. Not far from where I live now, for that matter. He left to go home before any of us, even though we were *all* pretty much blitzed by then. None of us, including him, should have even been out on the roads driving. This is where it gets really deep. Early the next morning, and I mean *very* early, he calls me, frantic, almost in tears. *Don't believe everything you read,* he said. I asked what he meant by that but all he said was *goodbye, I gotta go. Fast!* That night I hear on the news about a double murder in a New Jersey suburb. Two people had their throats slashed, apparently while they were sleeping. Those people were Al's parents. And, as far as I know, those murders have never been solved. Following our short, panicky phone call, he disappeared from the face of the Earth. It's really weird, though. I get Christmas cards every year from him, always postmarked from a different country and never with a return address. Never with a note of any kind. I didn't get one, however, this past Christmas which makes me wonder if he is still alive."

"That family certainly attracts murders doesn't it?" asked Devon Stone.

"Indeed, Devon," answered Tony Dunlap. "It makes me wonder if the current murder in question might be a link to the past. Obviously something that the police should handle. I'll say no more at this time because, frankly, what little facts I know are a bit vague."

"Hmm, interesting," said Devon, frowning.

Bankston Bruin sat up straight and shook his head.

"Okay, then," he said, slamming his hand down on the table with a loud wallop. "There's the title for your next book, Devon. *The Ghost Who Vanished.* You're welcome!"

Devon rolled his eyes and sighed. "Let's get back to the *real* reason I'm here and talk book tour, shall we? By the way, Tony, I love all those dust jacket concepts. The book here in the States will look more impressive and attractive than its U.K. counterpart. I've already selected my favorite."

"Let's go to lunch, Devon," interrupted Bankston, glancing at his watch one more time. "I don't know about you, but I'm starving. We have a lot of ground to cover and a nice meal and a drink or two will make it even more pleasurable. We'll be meeting with our lawyers back here again at two-thirty. Oh, you'll see a big ebony statue of Buddha when you enter the restaurant. It's over six hundred years old, I'm told. Be sure to rub his belly and make a wish. He'll bring you good luck."

Devon Stone will need it.

The rush hour traffic was driving *out* of Manhattan as Billy and Peyton were driving *in*. Billy drove his car down the ramp into the Lincoln Tunnel with ease, hardly tapping his brakes at all as they watched the heavy traffic flow out into New Jersey.

"Can you imagine doing this every day?" commented Peyton shaking his head. "I'd go nuts."

"Short trip for you, buddy," laughed Billy. "Short trip."

Billy was rewarded for his comment with a special finger gesture. They both laughed. Coming up out of the exhaust fume-filled tunnel, Billy guided his car up the ramps to the parking garage on top of the Port Authority Bus Terminal. Commuter buses, loaded to standing room only, drove out of the terminal heading to points west. He parked and then they both rode the escalators down to the main floor and headed out onto a bustling 8th Avenue.

"Let's see if he's back to his hotel yet before we go get something to eat. We may have to wait a while," said Billy, as they walked the few short blocks to the Algonquin.

As luck would have it, combined with perfect timing, the two men were at the front desk asking about Devon Stone when he happened to walk through the front door and across the lobby. He spotted his friends right away but stopped in his tracks. *Why are they here again?* he thought to himself.

They greeted each other with handshakes and friendly back patting.

"Don't tell me there's been another murder," Devon laughed.

Billy Bennett and Peyton Chase looked at each other.

"Well," Billy said hesitantly. "As a matter of fact, there has."

11

"I'll be the first to admit," Devon said staring at the newspaper that Billy had handed to him, "that many of my books are laden with convoluted plots, but *this* situation is beginning to make my head hurt."

He started reading the newspaper article to which Billy had opened. The irony of the headline, *GRIM MURDERS*, was not lost on any of the three men in the room.

> The recent murder in a Manhattan hotel of Morristown resident Brenda Barratt, 75, has the citizens of Dover on edge. Mrs. Barratt comes from a prominent Dover family, which had been part of this community's history for generations. Tragedy seems to have followed this family throughout the years. In 1903 Grover Sutton, Mrs. Barratt's father, loaned a painting by an obscure artist to the Dover Preservation Society. The deal was struck, and legal papers drawn up, that the Society would maintain and display the painting for fifty years, upon which time it would be returned to the oldest surviving member of the Sutton family. Earlier this year lawyers representing the Society met with Mrs. Barratt, seeking for the permanent ownership of said painting. The painting, titled Memento Mori *depicts a gruesome image of the Grim Reaper. Over the years, works by the once-obscure artist have gained much popularity, especially throughout the European art community and that particular painting was recently appraised at $1,000,000. The lawyers, the Society, and Mrs. Barratt have been at odds, with the murdered woman insisting that the painting be returned to her as the original deal states.*

To add to the tragedy of Grover Sutton's family, Mrs. Barratt's only daughter and son-in-law were brutally murdered in 1946. That crime has never been solved although it was thought, at first, that Mrs. Barratt's grandson, Alistair Stickle, committed the crime. Mr. Stickle vanished the night of the murders and has never been found, and is presumed dead. The sole remaining survivor, then, of Grover Sutton's family is Frances Wayne, 66, the widowed younger sister of Mrs. Barratt, who now resides in London, England.

Devon Stone stopped reading at that point. The article also contained a photograph of the contentious painting.

"Didn't you mention something about another murder a couple minutes ago?" he asked the two men.

"Yes," answered Billy, "just this afternoon, as a matter of fact. We heard it on the car radio as we were driving in here. It made the news because of the tie-in with the Barratt murder. The victim, this time, was the young director of the Dover Preservation Society. She just happens to have been the sister of the lawyer Brenda Barratt was having the hassle with. And, guess what? That painting," he said, pointing to the photograph, "*Memento Mori*, was stolen."

Devon Stone was silent for a moment, contemplating both the article and what Billy Bennett had just told him.

"If, indeed," he said, "the murders have anything to do with that painting...and I'm now certain they *do*...that newspaper article did the surviving sister a major disservice by announcing her name to the world. She now has a target on *her* back."

One hour earlier, and oblivious to the murders that her boyfriend Billy Bennett was discussing, Veronica Barron fastened her seatbelt. Following the announcement by the captain of her Pan Am flight from London, the plane was making its final approach into New York's Idlewild Airport. A shiver of excitement coursed through her body. She had told Billy that she would be flying back to the States at the end of the month, but she couldn't wait. Actually, there was no reason to wait, so she decided to surprise him and show up on his doorstep unannounced. She had no fear of catching Billy in someone else's arms in flagrante delicto. His best buddy, Peyton Chase, would have squealed on him by now. She giggled at the thought.

After deplaning, it took her a bit longer than she had hoped to get through customs but finally through, and with her passport stamped, she hurried to baggage claim, collected her luggage and headed out to the awaiting taxis at the arrivals gate. She carried two small suitcases. The larger pieces were being shipped back. Hailing her cab, the driver gave her a nod but then gulped when she gave him a New Jersey address.

"Don't worry," she said knowingly, "You'll make up for the lost fares you might get tonight by the tip I'll give you. I'm not stingy. And don't think you can take the longest route out of the city. I might be blonde but I'm not dumb."

And they both laughed as he pulled his cab away from the curb, tires almost screeching.

"Gentlemen," said Devon Stone, "my business here in the States is concluded for the time being. The deal has been struck regarding my upcoming book tour and I've approved the artwork for the book's cover. Their lawyers had me sign so many papers and contracts that I nearly got writer's cramp. I had intended to stay a couple more days for some research on that book I'm currently well into, but I need to head back to London. There's some unfinished business I must attend to before heading back here for the tour next month. I'm halfway through my next book and, after some conversation with my publisher here, I need to do some rewriting."

"What about the situation here?" asked Peyton Chase. "Any thoughts about the murders?"

"Peyton, my good man, I have too many fictional murders to worry about at the moment. I regret the dire situation. It's nasty to the core, I'm sure. But I do *not* want to get involved. I will, however, give that note that Brenda Barratt sent to me to Detective Lafferty before I go home. It'll be up to him what to do with it."

Earlier Devon had told both Billy and Peyton about the story from Tony Dunlap regarding the Ghost Army and Alistair Stickle. They had heard only faint rumors about the bizarre mission while they were serving overseas but they didn't know any of the particulars. They were quite surprised that Tony Dunlap would now be telling a civilian, and a foreign one at that, about the highly classified mission. Their minds were spinning —and in sync.

"We're taking the subway down to Katz's Deli, Devon. I promised poor starving Peyton here. Want to join us?" asked Billy.

"Thanks, but I'll pass," answered Devon. "I just had a huge luncheon with my publisher and I'm done eating for the day. I'm going to contact Detective Lafferty, invite him for a drink at the bar downstairs if he's available and then drop into bed with a plop. I'm beat!"

"I guess, then, there might be a chance we'll see you again in a couple months?" asked Peyton.

"Yes, there is that chance. Just, *please*, don't be telling me about any more murders," Devon chuckled in return. "Go. Enjoy whatever Katz's has to offer and good night. Goodbye. Au revoir. Bon soir. Tschüs! Sortez! Naten e mire! And while we're at it, allez vous en! Now, get out!"

Both Billy and Peyton laughed boisterously as Devon Stone led them to the door.

"Auf wiedersehen für jetzt und alles gute!" Billy exclaimed as Devon slowly closed the door behind them.

A devastated and frightened Jefferson Langston parked his car in his driveway and slowly walked up to his front porch. It was late, it was dark and a misty drizzle had just started. He had spent hours with the police and had to make the identification of his murdered sister. With his head drooped, the lawyer failed to see that someone was waiting for him in the shadows. As he stepped onto the porch, the figure moved.

"Jesus Christ!" he yelped. "You scared the shit outta me. What were you thinking?"

The figure moved forward, stepping out of the shadows, and Jefferson cocked his head to one side.

"Wait. You look familiar, do I…?"

His question was cut short by the sharp blade that swiftly sliced through his neck severing his carotid artery and tearing through his larynx.

~

"Your timing was impeccable, Mr. Stone," said Detective Lafferty, as he slid onto a bar stool next to the author. "You caught me at the precinct just as I was about to head out into the night with nothing on my agenda but a cold beer in my hand and *Dragnet* on television."

"Cold beer I understand," said Devon with a smile, "I haven't a clue about *Dragnet*. And I never watch television. It unnerves me."

Both men chuckled at that.

They toasted to each other's health, Devon with his favored gin and tonic and the detective with a frosty glass of Schaefer. Devon pushed a filled bowl of peanuts toward the detective and he immediately began shelling them, popping the nuts into his mouth and loudly crunching.

Devon couldn't help but notice the detective's attire. Lafferty was wearing a stylish, neatly pressed charcoal grey suit, a white button-down club collar shirt that had a very thin grey pinstripe, and a perfectly knotted burgundy, black, and dark grey diamond-pattern necktie. He removed his hat; a grey felt Fedora with a burgundy, black and white feather tucked into the black band, and placed it on the bar in front of him.

"I must say, Lafferty, you are without a doubt the best-dressed detective I have ever encountered."

The detective looked down at his suit and chuckled.

"My father has been the men's wear buyer at Bloomingdale's for years, Mr. Stone. I couldn't possibly afford my wardrobe without his deep discounts and benefits. Bet you thought I was a cop on the take, didn't you?"

"Never entered my mind, Lafferty," Devon Stone lied. *A fop on the take would be more like it,* he thought. "Never entered my mind. Bloomingdale's, you say? Exquisite store. Did you know that they were the very first retail outlet to use the escalator back in 1898 after it was first invented?"

"No, sir, I did not. How do *you* know that?"

"I'm a writer and I know things. I may have to slip you in as a character in one of my next books."

"If you do, Stone, please don't make me the killer!"

Both men laughed, and took long sips from their respective beverages.

"Now then, I have no idea where the Barratt case stands with you, Detective, as I'm sure New York being New York you have a rather full plate. But I wanted to give you this note that the unfortunate woman wrote and sent to me probably mere moments before she was slain."

He handed the short note to the detective and he read it carefully. Then he reread it.

"Hmm," he said wrinkling up his nose. "There are a lot of unsaid words in there, aren't there? Unanswered questions yet to be asked. Just what does she mean by time running out? Yes, I've done a bit of digging into the situation and I heard just a short while ago that there was a murder out there in Jersey today that may be linked in some way."

"Word travels fast, as that old cliché goes, doesn't it?" asked Devon. "I'm sure you and whatever police force there is in Dover will compare notes on this one. I guess considering that a citizen of one state was murdered in another state complicates the procedure."

"Yes and no," answered Lafferty. "We'll communicate and share information. This one is a strange one; I'll give you that. It's complicated, to say the least. Not like a good old cut and dried mob hit. We have had *more* than our share of those lately. Frankly, I don't recall anything quite like this in any of your books, sir. Any thoughts about this one? Will it work its way into a future Devon Stone thriller?"

Devon sighed deeply.

"No. And no," he replied succinctly. "I have too much going on right now. I simply want to back out of this. I got into it, as slight as it might be, by mere happenstance. Unfortunately, as we all know, one cannot unring a bell. I cannot unsee that blasted note. But I do *not* want to be involved any further in any way."

But it was too late for that. Way too late.

"Well," said Lafferty standing up to leave, "next time you're in town give me a call. I'll treat *you* to a drink or two at *my* favorite place around here. Actually, I have *two* favorite hangouts, one of them being McSorley's Old Ale House down in the East Village. Oldest Irish saloon in Manhattan. But I'll invite you to the other one that I think you might favor. You ever hear of Pete's Tavern down in Gramercy Park?"

REMEMBER YOU MUST DIE

"Can't say that I have," answered Devon Stone. "And it's one of your favorites for what reason?"

"History, Mr. Stone. History. Great atmosphere. And damn good drinks. Oldest operating bar in the city. And, being that you're a writer and know things, maybe you might want to know that it was O. Henry's favorite hangout. Did a lot of writing there, so I've been told."

"I shall definitely take you up on that offer, Lieutenant," Stone replied, downing his drink. "Remember, I won't forget now that you've mentioned it."

Lieutenant Lafferty chuckled and tipped his hat to Devon Stone as he started toward the door.

"That memory thing of yours is creepy, Stone. I'll just bet that it's gotten you *into* more trouble than *out* of it."

"You have no idea, lad. No idea."

12

Billy Bennett and Peyton Chase shared a decent-sized two-bedroom, one and a half bathroom apartment in a decades-old two-family house on quiet Baker Avenue, a half mile from the center of town. On days of good weather they would often walk to their gun shop. Aside from an updated kitchen, they enjoyed their spacious living room and a small dining room. For two *seemingly* rough and tumble bachelors, they kept very neat living quarters. The apartment was almost always spotlessly clean. Fearing that it might end up looking like something from army surplus, Veronica had volunteered to help decorate the place when the two men moved in. She kept the furniture to simple, clean Scandinavian lines. Meaning a lot of teakwood, and looking nothing like what their grandmothers would have used. They all agreed on a very masculine color palette of shades of brown, cream, grey, and green. The one somewhat feminine touch, albeit minor, were the chrome and vinyl chairs in the kitchen, matching the chrome and Formica table. Neither man liked the turquoise vinyl seats, but they graciously acquiesced. Peyton joked about the thin-lined grey, black, and white boomerang motif on the Formica tabletop, calling it childish scribble. Veronica ignored him.

Mostly older residents lived in the neighborhood and all the houses were dark when they turned onto their street off of West Blackwell Street. A few streetlights were lined among the large, old oak trees that leaned over the street, casting long shadows on the roadway. The two men lived on the ground floor beneath the owners, George and Betty Peer, both of whom were well into their seventies and retired every evening before 9 P.M. The one yearly exception being New Year's Eve when they could often stay awake at least until 10.

It was well past midnight when they drove toward Dover, still discussing the recent murders and the mystery surrounding the missing army man who had played a role in the Ghost Army. Every once in a while a belch, silent or otherwise, caused by the multiple cans of Dr. Brown's Cream Soda consumed along with their pastrami sandwiches, reminded them of their enjoyable meal earlier at Katz's. Halfway home Peyton Chase couldn't keep his eyes open and he leaned back into a comfortable sleep as his friend drove on in silence.

The light rain that had been falling earlier had slowed to barely a very faint mist and Billy turned off the windshield wipers. As he turned his car into the driveway along side of their house leading to the detached garage around back, his headlights quickly swept across their front porch from left to right. The shadows caused by the slats in the railing gave the eerie impression that they were moving.

"Did you see that?" asked Billy, awakening his slumbering friend.

"What?" asked Peyton. "Are we there yet? What did you just say?"

Billy turned off the headlights and slowed the car as he went down the driveway.

"We should have remembered to turn on the front porch light when we left this afternoon," Billy answered. "I swear I saw somebody up on the porch. Back in the shadows. Somebody hiding in one of those old chairs. This murder stuff has me on edge. We better play it very carefully, buddy. Who knows? Somebody might be after *us* now."

Peyton always carried his trusty Beretta. Billy was unarmed.

Billy stopped and parked the car, turning off the engine before he got to the garage.

"You come around on this side of the house," he said to Peyton as they both quietly got out of the car, leaving their doors open. "You've got the gun. I see a shovel over there leaning up against the house and I'll go around the other side from the back. You surprise the son of a bitch with your gun. If he jumps off the porch in the other direction I'll crown him with the shovel."

They cautiously crept in their respective directions. Peyton had his gun drawn and ready. Both men felt their pulses quicken. Almost like wartime. But who was the enemy *this* time? Did someone know that they had been meeting with Devon Stone?

Peyton slowly peeked around the side of the house. There was, indeed, someone on the porch, hunched over, back in the shadows. In the dim light thrown by a distant streetlight he saw Billy with the shovel raised above his head, ready to strike out. Peyton made an energetic lunge, landing on the porch with a loud thud, gun raised high, and shouted.

"Make one move outta that chair, asshole, and you'll be sayin' hello to Jesus!"

Suddenly awakened, Veronica Barron let out an ear-piercing scream.

Within minutes, one by one, front porch lights quickly flashed on up and down the street.

Billy Bennett dropped the shovel and came running to the front of the house and up the steps to the porch.

"Veronica? Ronnie? What the hell?" he exclaimed, his heart racing.

"What the hell is right!" Veronica shot back at him, her heart racing even faster. "I mean, where the hell have you two been? I've been waiting out here for hours. Your landlords aren't home, I don't have a key, I've had a very long flight and I'm exhausted. Sitting here alone in the dark I tried to stay awake but I couldn't. And you, Peyton Chase! What the hell was *that*? What kind of training were you given or have you forgotten everything already? Suppose I *had* been some kind of perpetrator waiting for you up here on the porch. You jump up here like a crazed idiot brandishing a weapon. And yelling like a banshee. I could have shot you dead before you even *mentioned* Jesus, you idiot!"

"You called me an idiot twice," Peyton responded, embarrassed.

"I may call you an idiot one more time tonight if you don't watch out," she said, almost laughing.

"Now, Billy Bennett, get *your* cute ass over here and kiss me...you idiot!" she said with her arms outstretched.

They embraced and held a kiss for a long time. A *very* long time. Peyton turned away, truly embarrassed and feeling a little awkward by the tenderness. He went back and closed the car doors that each of them had left open.

"I thought you weren't coming home for a few more weeks. I was expecting to go to the airport and greet you like the homecoming heroine that you are," Billy said, his heart rate coming back to normal.

"Sorry to spoil your plans, if you *really* had any," Veronica replied, bending over to pick up one of her suitcases. "I simply couldn't wait any longer. Now can we please go inside? I have a feeling that the neighbors may have called the cops because of your shenanigans a few minutes ago."

"It was *your* scream that probably did it," Peyton said somewhat sheepishly.

"Watch it, Chase, the word *idiot* is coming very close to being used again," she said with a sly wink.

Billy took the suitcase from her hands and picked up the other one as Peyton unlocked the door to their apartment. They went inside and Billy flicked on the lights.

"It's good to be back," Veronica said with a big sigh. "London was great. I certainly loved the theater and all my friends over there, but I missed the States. After that little…hmmm… shall I say *adventure* that we had last year, it'll be good to get back to the peace and quiet around here. I can do without the word *murder* for a long, long time!"

Billy Bennett and Peyton Chase turned and stared at each other.

13

Although both men were ruggedly handsome and caused women's hearts to flutter at a glance, Peyton was often considered the better looking of the two. Whereas Billy was more suave and always neatly dressed, Peyton was more muscular and appeared to be rough around the edges. A blue jeans and T-shirt kind of guy. With his perpetual smirk, dark brown wavy hair and his smoldering eyes, he always seemed to be hiding a secret. In a gastronomical way, he was. And Billy had reaped the rewards ever since sharing their living quarters. Between the two men, Peyton was the one who had developed into a very good cook. A talent that he really enjoyed.

Veronica awoke a few short hours after the rousing welcome on the front porch to the aroma of coffee drifting through the apartment. Billy must have gotten up and left the bedroom without disturbing her. She pulled a robe out of one of her suitcases, wrapped it around her, and headed off into the kitchen. Billy was sitting at the table reading the morning newspaper and Peyton was at the range, flipping perfectly browned, fluffy pancakes. Bacon was sizzling in another skillet.

"Well, good morning, cowboys," she said, stifling a yawn. "Aren't *you* the domestic one, Peyton? Smells fantastic."

"Sit, have a cup of Joe and the pancakes will be ready in a sec," Peyton said with a wide smile. "Oh, and welcome home. Somehow in all that excitement I forgot to say that last night."

They all laughed.

"I suppose," Peyton mused, "now that you're back home permanently, I should look for some other living quarters, right?"

"Don't be silly, you big goof," replied Veronica. "We're all adults here. I can't speak for Billy over there, but I say stay here for the time being. No need to rush into anything like that just yet. Who knows? *We* might be the ones to move out. So what if people might talk? Two guys and a gal.

Let 'em. Who cares? Besides, based on what I'm looking at and smelling at the moment we'd only have to hire you every morning to come back here to prepare our breakfast anyway. So stay."

"I agree," said Billy. "No complaints from me. Yet."

He hesitated for a few moments.

"You know, Ronnie, you said something last night about the peace and quiet around here. The word murder slipped into that part of the conversation as well."

Peyton, as his eyebrows suddenly shot up into an arch, looked up at him as he was talking. He almost wanted to shake his head as in "*no, don't go there*" but he didn't.

Twenty minutes later, with the Vermont maple syrup-soaked pancakes devoured, just a couple tiny dried slices of the bacon remaining on the platter, and the coffee pot now empty, Billy Bennett concluded the story about the murder of Brenda Barratt and the note that she had written to Devon Stone. He also included the parts about the murder of the director of the Preservation Society and the stolen painting worth one million dollars.

"Well," Veronica said as she pushed back her chair. "At that posh, old, expensive and snooty Plaza Hotel of all places? Never would have thought something like that could *ever* happen at that place."

The venerable Plaza Hotel, however, was not without murder in its past. A little-remembered fact is that there *had* been a scandalous (for the time) murder at the Plaza Hotel while it was under construction in 1906. Michael Butler, a 41-year-old ironworker, was struck by a heavy bolt and then set upon by a gang of ten other workers. They beat him unconscious and dropped him two stories to the ground. He was able to regain consciousness just long enough to identify his attackers before dying. *Murder in Mid-Air*, as the press had dubbed it, was a result of tensions between union and non-union construction workers.

"Well, well, well. And all of that within this past week, right?" asked an intrigued Veronica.

"Right," answered Billy.

"Has that poor woman had a funeral yet?"

"Actually," Billy responded, "I was just reading about that in the paper a few minutes ago. Her younger sister just flew over from London and the funeral is tomorrow. In Morristown."

"Hmm," said Veronica. "I think we should go."

"*What?*" Billy said agape, "What the hell for? What reason would *we* have to go?"

"I'm intrigued," Veronica replied.

"Ronnie," Billy said in disbelief. "We've already played that little Nick and Nora Charles game once."

"*Oh*, and wasn't it fun?" she laughed. "Exhilarating, frightening but fun, wasn't it?"

"No!" Billy said emphatically. "It certainly was *not!*"

Peyton, quickly grabbing one of the remaining pieces of bacon, leaned up against a kitchen counter and watched the banter, folding his arms across his chest while shaking his head.

"What time is the funeral?" Veronica asked.

"We are *NOT* going!" Billy almost shouted.

Billy Bennett and Veronica Barron stood a short distance away from the friends of the deceased as they offered their condolences and said their goodbyes to her sister at the gravesite in the Evergreen Cemetery. It was a beautiful spring day with cloudless skies and birds chirping happily almost mocking the somber occasion. The fragrance from the numerous floral arrangements, ranging from small to gigantic, bordered on overpowering. The casket had been lowered and people slowly drifted off toward their cars. Veronica, with Billy reluctantly following, approached the grieving sister.

"Mrs. Wayne?" Veronica asked solemnly. She had read the woman's name in the newspaper's obituary.

"Yes?" answered Frances Wayne as she dabbed a few tears from her eyes.

The woman was tall, slender, but obviously in great physical shape for someone in her mid-sixties. Raven hair cut into a stylish bob, she wore a deep purple jacket over a mid-calf black skirt and a white silk blouse. A large sparkling black spinel pendant hung from a white gold chain around her neck, with earrings to match. Her dark brown eyes were tinged with red from crying. Veronica instantly recognized the intoxicating perfume that she was wearing. And she couldn't take her eyes off that pendant.

Frances Wayne dapped her eyes once again, trying to remain stoical.

"We are so sorry for your loss," Veronica began, extending her hand. "Please accept our condolences."

Billy shuddered with how trite and artificial that actually sounded. He wished he could just disappear.

Smiling wanly, Frances Wayne took Veronica's hand and held it firmly. She stared at Veronica for a moment, and cocked her head slightly.

"This is my good friend Billy Bennett and I'm Veronica Barron, and we..."

"Wait," said Frances. "Veronica Barron? Oh, I know you! I *thought* I recognized you. I saw you in *Private Lives* at the Drury Lane a few months ago. Oh, my *heavens*. You were marvelous, my dear. But I can't believe you're here. I had no idea. Were you friends with my sister?"

"Well, no. Actually, we never met your sister."

Frances Wayne almost did a double take, not knowing how to accept that answer.

"No," Veronica continued, "we never met but we're friends with Devon Stone."

Frances Wayne cocked her head again and frowned.

"Am I supposed to know who *he* is?" she asked, a little perturbed by now.

"Well, perhaps not, Mrs. Wayne. He's an author and had a short conversation with your sister on their flight over from London several days ago."

"Oh," answered Frances Wayne haughtily, "I never, ever read murder mysteries. A waste of time in my opinion and most of them are so unrealistic and unbelievable. Folderol. So why then, exactly, are you here?"

She stood back, folding her arms and giving the couple a withering look.

"To be honest, even though we don't know a thing about you or the situation, our friend Devon is concerned that now *you* might be in danger."

"I'm incredulous," stated Frances Wayne rather bluntly. Her voice turned from warm and friendly to accusatory. "What in the hell are you talking about, Miss Barron? What in the *royal* hell?"

"Well, from what we've read in the papers, the murder of your sister and one other unfortunate young lady had something to do with a painting belonging to your family at one time."

Frances Wayne squinted her eyes and turned, looking at Billy.

"Is your friend here a lawyer?" she asked, nodding in Billy's direction.

"I am not, ma'am," Billy answered.

"Are you with the press?"

"I am not, ma'am."

"Then what in blazes do you hope to accomplish today by approaching me at my poor beloved sister's funeral? This is ghastly, rude, and bordering on obscene."

"But our friend Devon thinks that you might now have a target on *your* back, Mrs. Wayne. We just came here to implore you to be wary," answered Veronica, now almost in tears.

"Because of that wretched old painting? Ha! I nearly forgot about it until all hell broke loose among the vultures of the media. I have *no* desire to have it turned over to me now that my poor sweet Brenda is gone. That ghastly painting is as ugly as a porcupine's asshole, if you'll pardon the French. I don't care *how* much the damn thing is worth. Not to sound too pretentious, but I do not need, nor want the money. Let the library keep the damn thing."

"The Preservation Society," corrected Billy.

"Library. Preservation Society. Whatever." Frances Wayne said with a leer. "Tell your nosey friend, Darren…"

"Devon," corrected Billy again.

"Darren, Devon…whatever," Frances said, now seeming to have steam coming from her ears. "I'm sorry, and I'll try to make this sound as polite as I can considering the circumstances and the day I've had. While I appreciate the concern you seem to have, no matter *how* misguided it might be, I think you had a hell of a nerve coming here, butting into something you know absolutely *nothing* about. Now, please turn around, leave me to grieve in peace. And mind your own fucking business."

⌇

"Something's not right," said Veronica as they drove out of the cemetery and headed into afternoon traffic.

"You mean aside from her language? I *told* you that we shouldn't have come. *That's* what's not right," Billy answered, not only slightly mad but very embarrassed by the encounter.

"No, Billy, that's not what I mean. You didn't pick up on it, did you?"

"What are you talking about?"

"Oh, it was quick, but I certainly didn't miss it. It was like missing a cue, or misspeaking in the theater."

"I'm at a loss," said Billy, shaking his head and trying to pay attention to the congested traffic ahead.

"Well," said Veronica, clearing her throat. "She *appeared* to be totally unaware of Devon Stone or who he was. I told her that he was an author. I didn't tell her what he wrote. But she quickly said she didn't read murder mysteries."

"Oh," said Billy. "Well…okay, you're right. So? She may have suddenly remembered who he is. He *does* have a world-wide reputation, you know."

"Perhaps. And then when I said that Devon and her sister had a brief conversation on the airplane there was a sudden, strange look that flashed across her face and was gone in an instant. I read people very well, Billy, and I'm telling you that that woman is concealing something. Something's fishy here."

"You've been back home less than two days and look at the commotion you've caused already," Billy said, a bit more sternly than he really intended.

Veronica pouted, sticking out her lower lip. It may have been an act but, *dammit,* he thought, *she's cute when she does that.*

"I'm sure she was being honest when she said she didn't need the money. Her clothes were obviously haute couture and she was wearing Shalimar. Very expensive. *Very* expensive," said Veronica as she glanced out the window.

"How do you know *that?*" asked Billy.

"I *should* know. I spritzed myself with it at least once a week at the perfume counter at Harrods for the last two years. And that jewelry *didn't* come from Woolworth's."

Silence for a few minutes.

"Well, where do we go from here, Nora?" Billy said sarcastically, turning to stare at his passenger as he stopped for a traffic light. "Where *do* we go?"

Veronica chuckled.

"Well, Nicky, let's find out."

Billy Bennett didn't *want* to find out. But he feared that Veronica *did*.

They had not paid attention to the news report regarding the murder of a local lawyer, Jefferson Langston, which had happened the very night Veronica returned from London. They had yet to make the connection between that and Brenda Barratt.

The next afternoon Devon Stone settled back and fastened his seatbelt. His BOAC flight to London was about to pull back from its departure gate. He made a silent vow to himself to strike up a conversation with absolutely *none* of his fellow passengers.

14

Seven Years Earlier - December 3, 1946...

Alistair Stickle was drunk. He knew he probably shouldn't be driving but he did so any way. *I survived the damn war,* he thought in his drunken stupor, *surely I can survive Route 17.*

He had been drinking with his best friend Tony Dunlap and a few other former army buddies at a little unpretentious but popular bar just across the New York/New Jersey border in Rockland County near Tony's house. Unpretentious, because it resembled so many other little bars in the area, with nothing special about it. Even the flashing red neon sign above the small entrance lent to its simplicity and lack of imagination: BAR. Popular, because it was a destination for many underage teenagers from New Jersey who were of the drinking age, 17, in New York State but not their home state. It was dubbed *The No-Name* by the teens who frequented it on Friday and Saturday nights during their senior high school or early college years.

Alistair rolled down his driver's-side window to let the air refresh his mind and help with the queasiness in his stomach. It was cold and snow flurries blew in at times, chilling his face. Somehow it felt good. He turned up the volume on the car radio, hoping it would keep his mind alert. Nat King Cole singing *The Christmas Song* made him smile. Made him nostalgic. He missed the magic of Christmas. He forgot the atrocities of the recently ended war and remembered running downstairs on Christmas mornings in the past. His parents weren't the most loving of parents, but Christmases were always special anyway. His grandparents always made it even more special and showered him with abundant love and abundant presents. They spoiled him and he reveled in it.

After getting home from the service Alistair Stickle conveniently stayed at his parents' house in his old childhood bedroom while searching for more private living quarters. He had just recently found a tiny, tidy apartment and moved in. But now he suddenly grew very tired and felt his eyes droop. His new little apartment in Denville seemed a million miles away in his intoxicated mind. Realizing that he probably wouldn't be able to make it all the way home without having or *causing* a wreck, he decided to stop off at his parents' house in Rochelle Park to spend the night. It was late. He knew they must surely be asleep by now. But he had a key and would be very quiet. Perhaps, with luck, he could even leave early enough in the morning so that they wouldn't even know that he had been there.

He had no idea how true that was.

Ten minutes later he pulled his car into the short driveway of his parents' tiny Cape Cod-style house. The attached garage door was shut up tight, as he knew it would be at this hour. It was a quiet, middle-class neighborhood with an eclectic mixture of young families and the recently retired. *The newly wed and the nearly dead*, his father often joked sarcastically. He sat back in the car seat for a moment, his head still spinning. He rolled up the car window and stepped out into the cold night. There had been a couple inches of snow and he bent over, almost losing his balance, to make a snowball but thought better of it. If he had been paying attention he might have seen that there were tire marks in the snow on the driveway but he had pulled in up over them. The tire marks were not fresh, as they had been partially covered up anyway by the recently fallen snow. He giggled drunkenly and straightened up. The house was dark, as expected. His parents rarely stayed up past 10 P.M. But what wasn't *expected* was the fact that the front door stood wide open.

He cautiously walked up the three short brick steps to the small front porch.

What the hell, he thought. *Something's not right.*

He slowly stepped inside. Sobriety came rushing back.

"Mom? Dad?" he called out.

Silence.

"Hello?" he called louder.

The old Seth Thomas clock on the mantle in the living room chimed the quarter hour. It was 2:15.

The hairs on the back of his neck stood up. He was apprehensive as he moved slowly through the dark house, walking toward his parents' bedroom. He knew the way without having to turn on any lights.

He reached their door and cautiously looked in. He could see, even in the darkness, that they were in bed, side by side. But.

Something was *not* right.

"Hey, guys, I don't want to scare you. It's me."

Silence.

Not even the sound of breathing. Not even the sound of his father's obnoxiously loud snoring.

He stepped into the room, reaching around to switch on the light.

When he did so, he thought that he was going to faint, but he grabbed onto the doorknob to steady himself.

His parents lay side by side, their throats slashed, their blood staining the sheets and pillowcases. Almost not believing what he was seeing, he moved a bit closer and stepped on something. He foolishly reached for it, dropping it quickly.

A long, bloody knife.

His mind swirled, not from the alcohol but from the grisly scene and what he had just done. He had picked up the murder weapon. He fought an anguished scream but he couldn't fight the tears.

He went to the telephone and dialed O for operator. When she answered he told her to notify the police. There had been a double murder. He gave her the address and quickly hung up.

He panicked. Fear and confusion displaced logic. He ran out of the house, got into his car and drove away as fast as he could.

15

Present Day…

The conversation at the breakfast table the following morning between the three of them skirted the issue regarding the cemetery visit, but both Billy and Peyton relayed the story about Brenda Barratt's missing grandson. When Devon Stone had been with his publisher, he had been taken aback by the strange coincidence regarding the art director there, Tony Dunlap.

"Who is Devon's publisher?" asked Veronica.

"I don't remember," answered Billy. "Wait, maybe I do. I think he remarked about two bears being etched into the glass doors leading into their offices. The bears are part of the corporate logo. Bruin Publishing, that's it. I don't get the connection, though. I think the guy who runs the place is named Bruin."

"Well, I just happen to know," Veronica said with a smug look on her face, "that the word *Bruin* is Dutch for brown and, also, it's an English folk term for brown bear. I read books when I was a kid, believe it or not."

"What was it?" asked Peyton with a sly grin on his face. "*Goldilocks and the Three Bruins?*"

Both of the men snickered.

Billy chimed in, almost singing, "Maybe you sang that silly little song *The Bruin Went Over The Mountain. The Bruin Went Over The Mountain…*"

Both of the men snickered again.

Veronica stared at them, shaking her head.

"You two are idiots," she said.

"I'm getting used to that moniker," Peyton said, shrugging his shoulders, grinning like the Cheshire Cat.

The two men finished their breakfast, though not as sumptuous as the day before, cleaned the table and dishes and got ready to go off for another day at the gun shop.

"And what's on *your* agenda today, Ronnie?" asked Billy as he headed to the door. "Not going to rattle anybody's cages, I hope." And he laughed.

"Smartass!" she replied. "I think the rest of my stuff from London might be arriving today. A lot of unpacking ahead for me if it *does* come. Nothing exciting."

She waited until she saw Billy's car pull out of the driveway and head down the street, turning the corner. She slowly walked to the telephone and dialed 411.

Veronica Barron was about to go "over the mountain" to see what she could see.

The following day was Wednesday. Midweek Matinée Day for the Broadway theaters. Traditionally, little old ladies from the suburbs came into the city with other little old ladies for a day of shopping, lunching, and enjoying the latest Broadway hits. These suburbanite audience members, often referred to as "bridge and tunnel folk" by theater people, would never consider attending the theater in the evenings. Statistics show that there are more suburbanites attending a Wednesday matinée than any evening performance the entire week. Veronica Barron was well aware of these statistics.

Billy and Peyton were getting ready to leave together at 9:30 to open their gun shop. It was another beautiful day and they had decided to walk.

"Billy," Veronica called, as he was about to go through the door. "You're walking today? You won't need your car?"

"No, why?" he answered with trepidation.

"Well, I was thinking that perhaps I might go into Manhattan. I *was* going to go by bus, or maybe the train. Perhaps I might be able to get one ticket to see *Wonderful Town* this afternoon. Roz Russell visited with me backstage at the Drury Lane several months ago and she is *so* gracious. I'd love to see her and her show. It might be a sellout but perhaps I might get lucky. I also want to do some shopping. I miss Macy's. Actually, I miss the whole city. I just might stroll around for hours. Do you mind?"

He stared at her, squinting his eyes a bit, before answering. *What does she have up her sleeve now*, he thought.

"I have a car back there, too, ya know," Peyton interjected. "You didn't have to wait to use Billy's car."

Veronica scrunched up her nose.

"No offense, Peyton," she responded, "but your old jalopy is a stick. I've burned out a couple clutches and stripped too many gears in the past. So, Billy, I repeat. May I use *your* car and do you mind?"

Peyton rolled his eyes and Billy shrugged his shoulders.

"Sure," he responded, still leery of her intentions. "I mean, no, I don't mind at all. There should be plenty of gas in the tank. Just drive carefully. There better not be even one teeny, tiny scratch on my Oldsmobile when you get back. You *do* remember that we drive on the *correct* side of the road over here, don't you?"

She laughed, shaking her head.

"Silly!" she said, waving him off.

She watched out the front window as the two men walked down the street in animated conversation and turn the corner.

"She is definitely up to something," Billy said to Peyton as they walked. "Definitely."

"Really?" asked Peyton. "Sounds like typical girl stuff to me."

"Yeah, well," Billy answered, shaking his head. "She loaded that story with too much detail. Liars do that, ya know. They try to dazzle you with a multitude of facts and bullshit. Stuff that's possibly made up on the fly. I think that's what Ronnie is doing. Too many details."

"Why?" asked Peyton.

"I have an uneasy sneaky feeling that she's going to end up getting us into trouble."

"Us? What do you mean *us*?"

"Just you wait, buddy. Just you wait."

At 11:35 the elevator dinged on the 37th floor of the Empire State Building. The elevator operator named Otis announced the floor as he opened the doors. Veronica Barron smiled sweetly at him, stepped out, along with a half dozen other passengers, and looked around to find the Bruin Publishing Company's offices.

When she did so, she walked in and addressed the pretty young receptionist who smiled when she looked up from her desk.

"Good morning," Veronica said. "I'm Veronica Barron and I'm just a few minutes late for my appointment with a Mr. Tony Dunlap."

After a call from the receptionist, Tony Dunlap came out to the lobby, introduced himself to Veronica and led her back to his office.

His office was impressive and extremely colorful. At one end was a large drafting table set at a steep angle with a black goose necked architect's lamp attached at the top. Behind the desk was a large, long credenza with sets of brilliant Dr. Ph. Martins Dyes, and several sets of Prismacolor Pencils. An entire rainbow of Magic Markers stood like rigid soldiers in their well-designed holders. Large pads of tracing paper and layout paper leaned against the far end of the credenza. T-squares and triangles of various sizes lay on top of another credenza next to the drafting table. The wall at the opposite end of the room was cork, with pushpins stuck into it showing off various concepts for book jackets, photographs, and advertising posters.

"Oh," said Veronica when she spied a familiar name, "is that what Devon Stone's next book cover will be?"

"No," responded Tony Dunlap, "that's a reject. But that was *my* personal favorite. Devon picked this one." And he pulled the accepted concept from a long drawer in a flat file cabinet.

"Hmmm," Veronica said, sort of wrinkling up her face. "You know, I agree with you. I like the reject better."

"What can I say?" answered Tony, "Some of us obviously have better taste."

And they both laughed. Then Tony Dunlap turned serious.

"Miss Barron, I don't know what to say about your request. I was taken aback by your call yesterday but, as I told you on the phone, I haven't a clue about the nasty business with poor Brenda Barratt. And I am *really* confused as to why you would even contact me."

"But did you bring the cards?" asked Veronica.

Tony Dunlap hesitated for a minute and then he reached into the top drawer of the desk next to his drafting table.

"Yes, I did. I really don't know why I even kept these all through the years. I just felt so bad about my dear friend."

He laid five envelopes held together with an elastic band on his drafting table.

"And again, Miss Barron…"

"Please call me Veronica, Tony, okay?"

"Okay then, Veronica. I don't know what you hope to find with these Christmas cards. No notes of any kind. And, frankly, my curiosity has been aroused by your interest. Devon Stone said while he was here last week that he didn't want anything to do with this bizarre situation. Do you know something I don't? Has he changed his mind? I know he's back in London now, but he'll be back in another month or two for his book tour."

"No, I don't believe he's changed his mind but it's just a strange feeling that I have. A hunch, if you will. You *do* know, don't you, about the other murders regarding this situation?"

Tony Dunlap looked confused.

"You mean about Alistair's parents back in 1946? The possible reason he fled the country? Well, yes. Of *course* I know about those. I was the one who told Devon about them"

"No, no, I'm referring to the murders of the director of the Dover Preservation Society and her brother, the lawyer representing the Society."

Now Tony Dunlap leaned back in his chair and frowned.

"I guess I haven't been paying attention to the news, Veronica. I simply haven't had the time. No, I'm not familiar with *that* turn of events at all. I'm sure you're right, though. Something seems hinky, doesn't it?"

"I realize that I shouldn't even be butting into all this…and my boyfriend will scold me mercilessly when he finds out what I'm doing… but I'm intrigued."

"*Seriously?* Intrigued by murder, Veronica? And now several of them at that!"

"What can you tell me about the murders of Brenda Barratt's daughter and son-in-law…Alistair Stickle's parents?"

Tony Dunlap glanced at his watch.

"I'll have to make it quick and brief, Veronica. I have a luncheon meeting at 12 with an author who is a royal pain in the…sorry; I was about to use a very bad word. In a nutshell, I have a feeling that Al thought he might be accused of the crime and hence his rapid departure from…well, departure from Earth evidently. But the police interviewed all of us guys who were with him at the bar drinking that night. We all corroborated the time he left to head out into the night. Of course we all thought he was going home. The medical examiner had estimated the time of death and there was absolutely no way Al could have done it. The time it would have taken him to drive to their house would put him there several hours after the murders had been committed. But, unfortunately, he didn't stick around long enough to find out that little detail. It was known that he didn't get along that well with his parents, his father especially, but there is no possible way that I would ever believe he could commit such a heinous crime."

Tony handed the envelopes with the Christmas cards to Veronica.

"It's a good thing that I've lived in the same place since getting out of the army," Tony said, "Without a return address on these envelopes, I'm sure they wouldn't have been forwarded had I moved."

"There is one other thought I have on that subject," said Veronica as she glanced at the envelopes. "It just came to me as you were talking. Suppose he fled not out of fear of being accused but by the fact he may have known who the perpetrator was and feared for his *own* life?"

Tony Dunlap half-heartedly shook his head.

"Mmm, that's a possibility, but I'm hesitant to buy into that theory, Veronica. Al was too brave. I honestly doubt that he would run away because of that. I saw his bravery during the war. We may have been Ghosts, in a fake battalion, but we were still fighting a real war."

Her meeting with Tony Dunlap concluded, Veronica slowly walked up 5th Avenue and turned west onto 44th Street. She crossed over Broadway and she got a rush of excitement. Just down the street, on the right, was Shubert Alley. And across from that was her intended destination: Sardi's.

She didn't recognize the maître d', but she asked "Is Vince around today?"

"He is, ma'am. He is going around the tables…oh, there he is!" and he popped his arm up trying to get the attention of Vincent Sardi, Jr., the unofficial "Mayor of Broadway".

A distinguished-looking, balding man approached with his arms outstretched.

"Veronica, oh my, beautiful Veronica Barron. Welcome home, my dear. London's loss is our gain. Will you be on the boards again here sometime soon I hope?"

He kissed Veronica on the cheek as he held her hand in a firm grasp. He ushered her to a small table off to the side, out of the way of incoming guests.

"Time will tell, Vince. Time will tell. I hope so. I auditioned several months ago for the second lead in *Can-Can*. Didn't get it, though. They wanted someone younger."

And they both roared with laughter.

"Well, my dear, let me tell you about that one," Vincent Sardi said, after composing himself. "The young redheaded girl who got that part is knocking them dead during the tryouts in Philly. Stopping the show cold, I tell you!"

"Wow, now I feel sort of sad about losing out. It must be some fantastic part," answered a wistful Veronica.

"Ha!" Vincent hooted. "The main star of the show Lilo, a French prima donna, is furious. *Fuming!* That young dancer is getting more applause and attention than *she* is. Rumor has it that Lilo has insisted that the part be whittled down to practically nothing. Consider yourself lucky, then, Veronica."

"I'm keeping you from your rounds," Veronica said, looking around at the growing matinée-attending luncheon crowd. "Go, make your guests feel welcome. I just wanted to drop in to see if you were here today so I could say hello. Vince, you're the best. I'll be back soon. Count on it."

They kissed each other and she left the restaurant. Directly across the street was the Shubert Theater with the posters and marquee advertising *Can-Can*, opening on May the 7th. She went to the box office and purchased two tickets for the best seats for the first available Saturday evening. August 22nd.

"You did *what*?" exclaimed Billy Bennett, almost bellowing.

"I bought two tickets for…"

"That is *not* what I meant, and you damn well know that, Veronica!" stomped Billy Bennett, with a frightening scowl.

Veronica pouted.

"Not gonna work *this* time, kiddo," he said, arms crossed. "Stop pouting."

Peyton Chase stuck his head around the corner, glancing into the kitchen.

"Good night, kids, I'm gettin' outta here while the gettin's good. I'm going down to Sallie's for supper. I'll be back…whenever. Fight nice, you two." And he was gone in a flash.

Billy glowered at Veronica but she stood her ground.

"Billy," she began, "please hear me out on this. Maybe I jumped in too quickly but I think we might know some things —-or at least might find out some things—that could help the police in this case. Well, *cases*, as it turns out."

"You don't think the police detectives are doing their respective jobs here? But the big *main* question I have, Ronnie, is *why*? Why the hell should we even get involved? More to the point, why should we even care? We do *not* know any of these people. I simply do *not* understand your fascination with this."

Veronica apparently ignored his questions.

"I think perhaps the police, and Devon too, for that matter, might be missing a whole different side to this mystery," said Veronica deep in thought. "Listen, at first we all probably thought the lawyer and his sister were the devious ones. Not sure if murder had ever entered their minds… we'll never, ever know *that*. Then *they* were killed. Devon said that the note Brenda Barratt wrote to him mentioned about some thinly veiled threats. Yes, the Preservation Society came to mind first, didn't it?"

"Yeah," answered Billy half-heartedly, still perturbed.

"But let's take this further back. The police are more than likely focusing on the present. Perhaps they should be focusing on the past. In the theater we do different line readings during rehearsal. Trying to get new meanings into simple words. Perhaps even developing backstories for the characters we create and play on stage. We have forgotten one whole aspect of this mystery. Participants we haven't even considered."

"And that is who, Sherlock?" asked Billy petulantly, folding his arms across his chest.

"The family of the artist who did that painting, *Memento Mori*," Veronica answered.

"What?" Billy asked. "Why or how?"

"Well, think about it, Billy. We don't know how Brenda Barratt's father came into possession of that painting. Maybe there was something unscrupulous about the deal fifty years ago. Who knows? We can assume that the artist is long dead. More than likely he *is*. After all, he was an old man fifty years ago. But perhaps his descendants aren't. They heard about its recent appraisal and want to regain possession of it, no matter by what means."

Billy mulled that over for a few minutes, pacing around the kitchen table.

"Okay," he began. Stopped and thought about it for another few moments. "But what was your point in going in to see that guy at Devon's publisher? How does *he* figure into the scenario?"

"Well, only as a bystander to the past, so to speak," answered Veronica, feeling that now Billy was beginning to see her side of things.

He wasn't, though.

He was simply letting her act out her investigative prowess in hopes that it would wither away when actual facts about the case came into focus.

Veronica ignored his dismissive attitude.

"Brenda Barratt's grandson, Alistair Stickle, sent Christmas cards to his army buddy, this Dunlap guy, every year following his disappearance. From a different country every year. No notes, just season's greetings. Now, *he* may be dead too, for all we know. But then again, maybe he's not. Obviously he can't be doing the recent murders...unless he's back in the States. Tony Dunlap doubts that, though. *Wherever* Stickle might be, he could possibly be in danger now as well. Brenda's sister poo-pooed us when we cautioned her but she, too, just might be the next victim."

"But unless he makes his appearance, we have no way of knowing where the grandson might be if, indeed, he's still alive," said Billy, almost getting confused by all the thoughts swirling around in his head.

"I know," said Veronica, "but Tony Dunlap gave me the Christmas cards and their envelopes today. We can see where the missing man has *been*, at least."

Billy Bennett stood back, folded his arms across his chest yet again, and leaned against the kitchen counter.

"You're not really an actress, are you, Ronnie? You can come clean. I won't blow your cover. You're in the FBI, aren't you? Be honest."

"Don't be a blockhead," Veronica giggled. "Not a chance. Besides, they don't allow singing and dancing there."

16

Frances Wayne was glad to be back home in London. Aside from all the emotions surrounding her trip, she felt physically drained. She gathered up all the sympathy cards and notes of condolences that friends had sent and threw them in the trash. Some of which had remained unopened. She had gotten rid of all the floral arrangements before leaving for the States to attend her sister's funeral. She realized that there were still many things to be settled regarding Brenda Barratt's estate, but expected that a slew of lawyers would be calling within a few days and probably a trip back to the States would soon follow. Actually, she had no idea what else that might entail. If, indeed, Brenda's grandson, Alistair Stickle, was still missing and presumed dead, she, then, would be considered the sole surviving relative. Soon after the death of her husband several years before, Brenda Barratt had sold her big house in Dover and had currently resided in a large, expensive apartment building on the outskirts of Morristown, New Jersey. And regarding that estate? Frances Wayne was certainly very well aware that a particular painting was involved. That was where things had gotten dicey. And deadly.

She went to her telephone and dialed. It was the same number she had dialed at least half a dozen times since morning. She hung up after twenty rings.

"Damn!" she exclaimed out loud to herself. "Why the hell doesn't he answer?"

Devon Stone had been back home on Carlingford Road in the Hampstead section of London for three days and he still hadn't recovered from the thoughts of the murder at the Plaza Hotel. As much as he wanted to get it out of his mind, that note from Brenda Barratt haunted him.

The *what if's* taunted him. What if she *had* contacted him that night? She might not have been murdered. What if they *hadn't* struck up a conversation on the plane? He'd never even know about all this craziness.

He opened the front door to collect the mail from his little box on the porch. A stack of letters and a couple magazines. He took the lot in hand, fixed himself a late afternoon gin and tonic and climbed the three flights to his rooftop garden. As he walked to a chair in the center of the garden a flock of homing pigeons swooped low overhead, coming to rest on the coop of his neighbor, one rooftop to the south.

"Good evening, Chester," he called out, waving his free hand.

"Cheers, Devon," his neighbor called back as he went about feeding his birds.

Devon Stone plopped down in his chair, raised a silent toast to whomever, and sipped his beverage.

He made a quick scan of the mail he had brought up the stairs with him. A few pieces of junk mail. A magazine to which he had forgotten to cancel the subscription. And a plain white envelope, hand written, with only his name on the front and no address, no return address, and without a stamp. Someone obviously had placed it in his mailbox personally; either before or after the mailman had arrived. He tore open the envelope and unfolded the letter-sized paper inside. He frowned. There were only two hand-written words on the paper, placed right in the center of the page: *Memento Mori.*

He unlocked his front door and as he opened it, stepping in, he heard his telephone ringing. Matteo Amato didn't rush to answer it. He figured that if it were important enough, whoever it was would call back. He headed toward the kitchen to put his recently purchased groceries away. While doing so, he uncorked a bottle of Franciacorta that had been chilling in the refrigerator for the several days that he was in the United States. A loud pop was followed by a smile on his face. He poured himself a fluted glass full of the bubbly beverage and toasted to his own success. *Partial* success, he realized, but soon everything would be over. His endeavors over the years were never met with failure.

But his success rate would soon change.

Thirty minutes later, with the bottle now empty, the telephone rang again. He was in no hurry but after six rings he picked up.

"Pronto," he said.

He listened patiently.

"Yeah, yeah," he said with a smirk on his face. "Of course that was me. I took care of them. No doubt you heard about it on the news, right? I stayed a day or two longer than I had planned, but I had to do a bit more investigating. I want to make sure we take care of all possible loose ends, you know?"

The caller spoke at length.

"Hmm," he answered, "as I already told you, we *weren't* able to hear what she told him on the plane. She never even noticed us when she boarded. I expected that, though. We kept our heads down and her eyesight is horrible. But I don't plan to take any chances. I already know where he lives. I left a...shall we say a friendly little note for him. Plus, I think we should be counting on the very *real* possibility that Stickle is dead and has been for years."

He listened some more.

"I know, I know," he responded. "So, I fucked up back then. You don't have to keep reminding me over and over again, for chrissakes! You're like a broken record. But that was years ago. Mistakes happen. But what's the big deal? Actually worked out in our favor in the long run anyway, right? I'll take care of it, if need be. But I honestly think he's already dead. If not, where the hell is he?"

The caller said something that made Matteo Amato laugh.

"Is *that* who she was?" he asked. "Well I'll be damned. You were so friendly at first, and then from where I was standing it looked like the conversation turned sour in a hurry. She had a hell of a nerve approaching you at your sister's funeral. When I head back I'll see what I can do about them. Yeah, her and her boyfriend, too. Remember what I said about loose ends."

They stood, both naked, by the large open window overlooking the crashing surf two stories below. A soft, warm breeze ruffled her long blonde hair. The gossamer curtains fluttered and caressed their firm bodies. She was gently

87

leaning back against his smooth, chiseled chest and she could feel his arousal pressing against her buttocks.

"I do love you, you know," she whispered softly as she looked out toward the sea.

He was silent for a moment. Unconvinced.

"I love you, too, Cassandra, but you've lied to me haven't you?" asked Sebastian.

He already knew the answer and didn't wait for her to reply. She would surely lie again anyway. She had betrayed him for the last time.

He cautiously wrapped his left arm firmly across her upper torso, pulling her back even closer onto his chest as he slowly slid the long stiletto into the side of her body, between her ribs, puncturing a lung. She hardly struggled. He could feel her warm blood begin to ooze across his right hand as she...

The telephone ringing interrupted Devon's reading of the book by a new, young author. His London publisher, in hopes of getting a favorable review for some blurbs on the dust jacket, had sent the pre-publication copy of *Tell Me No Lies*, to him. He was more than grateful for the interruption. He found the writing pedestrian and overwrought, the characters one-dimensional, the plot preposterous and the author's knowledge of human anatomy laughable.

The phone rang for the second time as he placed the book on his desk. Devon answered after the third ring but his *"Hello?"* was greeted by a momentary silence and then a click as the caller hung up.

Fifteen minutes later someone rang Devon Stone's doorbell. He was just coming down the stairs from his office and was quick enough to see a man running down his front steps when he opened the door. A small, corrugated cardboard package, no more than perhaps twelve inches square, had been placed on the doormat. The man turned as he reached his awaiting car and smiled back up at Devon. *Why does that man look so familiar?* Devon thought.

"Buon viaggio," the dark-haired man called out, laughing, as he hopped into his car and quickly sped away.

The mechanism that was Devon Stone's remarkable and unfailing memory began to spin. Not having far to go, it stopped spinning when it reached a recent date less than two weeks ago: April 2 and at an altitude of 25,000 feet. The man had been one of the fellow-passengers in first-class on his flight into Manhattan. He had been sitting in the seat furthest back in that section. He glanced down at the package and frowned. He leaned over to pick it up but stopped when he heard a muffled but very distinct ticking sound.

His eyes widened and Devon Stone jumped back inside his house, slamming his front door shut just as the package exploded.

17

The sun slowly made its daily appearance over the eastern horizon and cast its blinding rays across the southern Pacific waters. A Dark-backed Imperial Pigeon took roost in a sheltering tree outside of an isolated hut. She ruffled her feathers and called out a morning greeting of her distinctive cooing. *Whuup…whuup…*

But there was no response. No one called out to greet her in return. The hut was vacant.

18

"Okay, now," said Veronica as she laid out the Christmas card envelopes in chronological order on the kitchen table. "Let's try to figure out his route. There might not be any logical pattern, but perhaps he's moving in a particular direction for some reason. Or not."

They looked at the postmarks and laid them out on the table from left to right, the oldest date to the most recent. Billy still didn't want to get involved with the mysterious doings. He was hesitant to play Veronica's game of *Where's Alistair*, but he decided to placate her, at least for the time being.

"We know that Alistair Stickle was discharged from the army in 1946. Late in the year, evidently, being that he vanished in early December. So there was no Christmas card that year. The card dating 1947 was postmarked in Italy. 1948 he was in Greece."

She and Billy tried to read the very faint postmark from 1949 and with careful scrutinizing determined that it was from Egypt. The postage stamps depicting the Great Pyramids of Giza were a clue. By 1950 Stickle had moved on to New Zealand.

"He seems to be moving from west to east," mused Veronica almost to herself.

They both looked at each other and shrugged when they read the postmark from 1951, the last card sent to Tony Dunlap.

"Where the hell is Mauritius?" asked Billy.

At that precise moment, fifteen thousand, nine hundred and eighty-eight miles away as the crow flies, Alistair Stickle was fastening his seatbelt. His Qantas flight from Sidney, Australia to the United States was about to depart.

PART TWO
A GHOST STORY

"Where large sums of money are concerned,
it is advisable to trust nobody."

———

AGATHA CHRISTIE

19

May 6, 1944…
Somewhere in Normandy, France. One month before D-Day.

"Hey, Al," Tony Dunlap called, "give me a hand here, will, ya?"

Alistair Stickle, bare-chested, ran over to his buddy who was trying to patch a leaking inflatable tank. The large, albeit fake vehicle flopped ridiculously to one side and would have looked totally puzzling to the enemy in the sky.

Tony applied a rubber patch and Alistair used an air compressor to right the vehicle once again.

"Crazy, huh?" asked Tony, shaking his head. "I guess this ruse is really working. Who woulda thought? Coulda fooled *me*!" he laughed. "Thanks, Al. See ya later."

Alistair Stickle went back to hanging "fake" laundry along a long clothes line making it appear from the air that there were countless dozens of soldiers at this base. Out of the corner of his eye, he caught another soldier…well, another "ghost"…wandering around a short distance away with a large sketchpad in his hand.

"Hey, whatcha got there, pal?" he called out.

The other man stopped, smiled and walked over to him.

"Capturing some sights and subject matter for some future paintings I hope," answered the man. "Assuming that I survive this friggin' war."

Alistair laughed.

"We'll survive. Just think positive, for fuck's sake," Alistair answered back. "As long as our inflatables here don't explode in our faces."

They both laughed.

"Hi, I'm Alistair Stickle," he said reaching out to shake the artist's hand. "But just call me Al."

The good-looking, dark haired young man grasped Alistair's hand, shaking it firmly, and cocked his head slightly. Alistair Stickle was the most handsome man he had ever seen.

"I'm Matteo Amato but, please, just call me Matt. That's what my friends call me."

Matt turned his sketchpad around. "Wanna see?" he asked.

"Wow," said Alistair, "I'll be damned. That's *me!*"

Matteo Amato laughed.

"So glad you recognized it. I've been sketching a lot of guys around the base. And landscapes too. When and if I ever get back to class I'll turn these into real paintings. Gorgeous countryside around here, you know, despite this little war thing that's going on."

"Did you say 'get back to class'? You're a student, then, I assume?"

"Yep, I was a senior at Parsons before Uncle Sam came calling."

"Parsons? Is that the Parsons School of Design in Manhattan by any chance?" asked Alistair.

"That's the one," answered Matt.

"Great school," replied Alistair, "I'm a graduate of Cooper Union myself, just a few blocks south of you guys. I majored in graphic design and advertising. So did my friend Tony over there," he said, pointing back to Tony Dunlap. "Should I assume that you're majoring in the fine arts?"

"You got it!" smiled Matt. "I got inspired when I was a kid by my nonno…oops, I'm sorry. My grandfather, that is. Sometimes I let an Italian word or two slip out. When I was growing up with my family back home in New Jersey that's all we spoke. My grandparents were from quote-unquote the old country."

"So your grandfather is an artist, too, you say. Is he famous, or anything?"

"Oh, good grief, no. Not yet, unfortunately," answered Matt. "He went up to that great Heavenly art studio in the sky while I was still in high school. He has a small following and I've seen it begin to grow slowly. Tragically, though, years after he had passed away. Hey, just like Van Gogh, right? Sold only one stinkin' painting while he was alive and now they fetch small fortunes."

"I'll keep my eyes open for his work. What was your grandfather's name?"

"Ha! I wouldn't hold my breath about them becoming known. Oh, his name was Matteo. Matteo Amato. I was named after him and I feel honored. He painted great work. Intricate, elaborate detail but dark, weird stuff, man, *really* weird. He seemed to have a strange fixation on death. He painted several paintings of frightening-looking skulls, dead animals, dead people, and even the Grim Reaper, if you can believe it. He also preferred to paint pictures of vases filled with *dead* flowers instead of living, colorful ones. My parents thought he was crazy. Perhaps he *was*. But I sat with the old guy in his studio and watched as he painted. I studied his technique. He had a great eye for detail, that's for damn sure. I loved that man. I inherited his talent, I guess. Well, part of it anyway. He and I had a very special bond. We understood each other."

"Oh, pal," said Alistair Stickle, "I can relate only too well with that. My parents weren't all that enthused when I went into my graphic design career. My father, especially, thought it was a career for sissies. But my grandparents, my grandmother in particular, supported every dream I ever had. She loves the arts. Has quite a nice collection. She can be a bit of a free spirit at times but she's the most beautiful woman I've ever known. Brenda Barratt...my angel. My guardian angel."

Matt smiled a wistful smile.

"That's great to have so much love there for your grandmother. Almost brings tears to my eyes. Seriously. I'm not kiddin' ya. I miss having that. There wasn't so much love in *my* family, sorry to say. Never was. Ever. A lot of hatred and anger, but I don't know what for! I'm talking too much. Hey, we just met and I'm unloading on you. Sorry, man. I gotta go. Maybe we can catch up at mess and talk further. Get back to work. We have some Nazi bastards to fool!"

They parted, waving goodbye to each other, and Alistair turned, catching up with Tony Dunlap.

Matteo, nicknamed Matt, walked in the opposite direction; sketchpad and charcoals ready for some more drawings. And with thoughts of Alistair Stickle in his head.

Amato. Matteo Amato, Alistair thought to himself. *Amato. Why does that name sound so familiar to me?*

He stopped in his tracks. He suddenly remembered.

20

Present Day...

Thrown forward by the blast as he ran from his front door, Devon Stone slid on his chest across his slick hardwood floors, scraping the floor with his belt buckle and banging his head against the base of the banister for his staircase. Large chunks of wood from his front door whizzed over his body, crashing into his hallway walls. He heard the tinkling of glass as shards from his shattered front windows rained down onto the floor. His ears were ringing from the intense explosion and, moments later, he thought he heard the sound of a man's voice. He was still dazed and the voice seemed to come from a distance.

"Stone! Stone?" called the voice. "Stone? My god, man, where are you? Are you alright?"

Chester Davenport, his next door neighbor (and retired Director of MI6), stepped through the smoking pile of rubble that was now the entryway into Devon's house. He saw Devon lying prone and unmoving on the floor and rushed to his side.

"Bloody hell," said Devon groggily as he leaned up on his elbows, lifting and turning his head to look at his friend. "If the blackguard didn't like my last book couldn't he have at least just written a nasty note?"

～～～

Four hours later, with his house cordoned off by the police as a crime scene, the windows and doorway boarded up as best as possible until the team of repairmen could arrive, questions asked and answered, Devon Stone, with a knot on his forehead and a throbbing headache, sat facing his typewriter. An empty piece of paper in front of him and smoke with the aroma of cannabis swirling around his head. He drew in on the freshly rolled joint and held it for a few seconds, slowly exhaling the smoke through his nostrils and leaning his head back. His concentration was anything but focused. The thoughts of the fictitious murderer about which he was currently writing intermingled with the thoughts of the real-life murderer –- or murderers—who may have followed him back to England. But who and why?

He picked up that handwritten note for the hundredth time and examined it. Remember you must die. *Memento Mori.* Two simple words in Latin. And with a couple different meanings: one ominous, one benign. Was it meant as a threat? As in *you must die* and *I'm going to kill you!* Or does it simply mean that *remember, we must all die eventually and death is inescapable.* How often, really, do we ponder our own mortality? Surely the young do not. How often do we stop to realize that from the moment we are born we are heading toward an inevitable and eventual death? Every day, after all, is a crapshoot. This fact of life (or death) becomes more of a reality the older and wiser we get. The best we can hope for is that we will die peacefully in our sleep. The worst? That we'll get blown to bits at our own doorstep.

He inhaled once again, holding the smoke briefly. Exhaling he thought about the more benign meaning of the phrase. The cannabis was making him a bit lightheaded and more than a bit philosophical. Devon Stone was well aware of the expression *Memento Mori.* He knew that it had been conceived by the philosophers of classical antiquity and had been around since medieval times. In writings, artwork and even architecture. If people would focus on the knowledge that death is inevitable, would they try to lead as purely honest and upstanding lives as possible? *Naïve thinking. Too bloody naïve,* he thought. *We're not all altruistic saints, of course. Nor are we all sinners.* Will they concentrate on taking advantage of all the opportunities that life presents to them? *That's a good thing,* he thought some more.

But he knew that this note was *not* meant as a good thing. It was *not* benign. It *was* a threat. A distinct threat, because those same two words, *Memento Mori,* had been scribbled on top of the box that had exploded at his doorstep mere hours before. Already several people have been murdered with those two words in Latin taking center stage.

How and why then has he been connected to the murder of Brenda Barratt aside from merely chatting with her for no more than fifteen minutes on an airplane?

He mulled it over and began putting a few rudimentary pieces together. His writer's vivid imagination, combined with his extraordinary memory and cannabis, started forming a potential scenario. Farfetched, to be sure, but he'd consider it possible.

One of the other passengers on that flight from London to New York must have been following Brenda Barratt without her being aware, he thought. *That person was extremely concerned about what Brenda had told him. And that was the man who had left the bomb. He had called out the equivalent to "bon voyage" in Italian as he ran back down the steps to his car. But was he acting alone?*

Devon stopped to put his thoughts together some more. He remembered that a female passenger was sitting next to that man.

My name was brazenly blasted in the newspapers about my connection to the crime, he continued thinking, *and now they want to make sure I don't live to tell the authorities any more than I have already. But I don't know anything. Brenda Barratt told me absolutely* nothing *that would or could implicate anyone of any crime.*

He stopped thinking.

"No, no, no!" Devon Stone exclaimed out loud, pushing back from his typewriter and shaking his head. "That just seems to scream cliché to me. Oh, no. I would never put that rubbish in any one of my books. My readers wouldn't buy into it, surely. That is simply *too* outlandish."

He leaned back in his chair and inhaled once again holding the smoke longer this time.

~~~~~

"Could this situation get any more outlandish?" Peyton Chase asked as he handed the morning newspaper article to Veronica and Billy. "Agatha Christie could work wonders with this one. Or Devon Stone."

Veronica leaned over Billy's shoulder as they read the article together. The piece started out by recounting the murders of both the director of the Dover Preservation Society and her brother, a lawyer. And then the weird part started:

> *Authorities were mystified yesterday by the sudden reappearance of the stolen painting,* Memento Mori, *by the late Italian artist Matteo Amato. Following the artist's sudden rise in popularity over the years, especially throughout Europe, the painting was recently appraised at the staggering sum of $1,000,000. It had mysteriously disappeared following the murder of Allyson Langston. While the Preservation Society has been closed pending the ongoing murder investigation, a large securely wrapped package containing the missing painting was found leaning up against the front doors of the facility yesterday morning. The painting appears to be unharmed and will be rehung in its place where it has been for the past fifty years. Authorities are refusing to...*

And that's where they stopped reading.

"I repeat," said Veronica Barron staring at Billy, "Something's not right."

"I repeat," said Billy Bennett staring at Peyton Chase. "She's gonna get us into trouble."

Tony Dunlap had bathed, shaved, and dressed before joining his wife in their cozy kitchen for breakfast.

"Hurry up, boys," he called to his two young sons. "You're running late. I'll drop you off at school before I hit the train station."

The Dunlaps lived in Suffern, New York, a bedroom community in Rockland County. Their three-bedroom, one bath Cape Cod had been built in the early 1940s and was beginning to feel cramped as their children grew. Tony had lived there before getting married and really hated that they might have to move into larger quarters before too long. The ride, by rail, connecting Suffern to Manhattan was only 34 miles but would take over an hour, making twenty-two stops along the route. Passengers would then detrain at Pennsylvania Station, an easy five-minute walk to his office at Bruin Publishing in the Empire State Building.

A cup with his first coffee of the day was about to hit his lips when the telephone rang. He frowned and glanced at his watch.

"What the hell?" he said. "Too early for *good* news. Who died?"

His wife shook her head and laughed.

"You're an old worry-wart," she said as she answered the phone.

She listened for a brief second.

"Yes, this is the Dunlap residence." A pause. "Yes. Yes he is, just a minute, please."

She turned and held out the phone to her husband. She shrugged her shoulders.

"Hello?" Tony said as he brought the cup to his lips for another sip.

"Tony?" asked the caller.

"Yes," answered Tony.

"Don't pass out, buddy. This is Al. Al Stickle."

Tony Dunlap dropped the cup, splattering coffee as it shattered on the linoleum floor.

21

Tony Dunlap was at a loss for words. Where to begin? He stretched out the long cord from the phone and sat in a kitchen chair as his wife cleaned up the floor.

"Oh, my God! What the hell…where the hell…?" he stammered.

"I expected, Tony, that hearing my voice and hearing my name after all these years would come as a shock to you. I'm sorry, my friend. But the time has come. Tragedy has brought me home. Just as a tragedy drove me away."

"There are *so* many questions, Al, so damn many questions," Tony said, finally regaining somewhat of his composure, although he could feel his heart racing like a Thoroughbred to the finish line. In rapid fire, he shot out the questions. "Where have you been? Are you back in the States? Where are you now? *How* are you?"

Alistair Stickle laughed.

"Slow down, Tony, you'll drop dead of a heart attack if you're not careful."

There was a long, silent pause.

"Yes, I'm back in the States. My flight got in late last night and I'm exhausted. But I was eager to make contact with someone and you were the first I needed to speak with. A confession first. I have been travelling with a fake passport for the past seven years. I have to be careful now that I'm back home. I know that there are no statutes of limitations for murder so I'm still a wanted man. I assume so, anyway. But I swear to you, I did *not* kill my parents."

"Before you go any further, Al…and you'd better damn well go further, *much* further…although the case regarding your parents' murders *is* still an open one, the police came to the conclusion that you could *not* have committed that crime. That being said, however, you fleeing the scene

107

and obviously leaving the country using a faked passport are other matters entirely."

Again, another long, silent pause.

"I was stupid," said Alistair Stickle with a sorrowful voice. "I panicked. It was an idiotic and foolish thing to do. Although I feel really certain I know who *did* kill my parents. The tragic part of it is that I believe it was a case of mistaken identity. It was probably dark and I think the killer thought he was killing *me*."

A week had gone by since Veronica Barron first met Tony Dunlap at his office. Billy and Peyton made a secret vow with each other to not bring up the subject of murder –*anyone's* murder—to Veronica. They hoped that she would sort of forget about it. At least for a while. There were no more news reports about the case and perhaps, just perhaps, the police might be closing in on a person or persons of interest. The two men went about their normal daily activities of running their gun shop and razzing each other whenever possible.

But Veronica had *not* forgotten about the crimes. Not by a long shot.

"Tony, obviously I don't know where you work after all these years. Is it still in Manhattan by any chance?" asked Alistair Stickle.

"It is," answered Tony Dunlap, still not fully recovered from the shock of hearing his friend's voice. "I work in the Empire State Building. Perhaps you know it?"

Alistair Stickle laughed.

"Still somewhat of a smartass, aren't you, Tony? I'm staying at the old Hotel Claridge on 44th and…"

"Oh, I know exactly where *that* is," answered Tony. "My two little boys love to stand across the street from it and watch that guy on the Camel Cigarettes billboard blow those big smoke rings out across the street."

"I plan on sleeping for most of the rest of the day," said Al, "but would it be possible, then, for you to meet me in the hotel bar when you get off work tonight?"

"Yeah, sure, Al. I'm still in a state of shock but I'm sure to recover by then. I have a hectic day ahead, but I can be there shortly after six. Will that work?"

"Sure will, but if I'm not there by then, come up to room 219 and pound like a crazed person on the door. I may not have awakened yet from my long day and night of traveling."

They ended the call and Tony Dunlap sat with his mouth agape, telephone receiver still just dangling in his hand.

"Well," said his wife. "Now the boys *will* be late for school and *you've* missed your train. What the hell was *that* all about?"

"Lynda, you're not going to believe it. A ghost has returned from the dead."

Shortly after six that evening Tony Dunlap walked up Broadway toward the Hotel Claridge. He glanced up at the famous Camel Cigarette billboard and chuckled to himself. Aside from blowing gigantic smoke rings every four seconds from a piston-driven diaphragm, the tag line under the brand name read *I'D WALK A MILE FOR A CAMEL*. He had just walked half a mile for a ghost.

Despite having seen the Hotel Claridge and the popular billboard from the *outside* possibly hundreds of times in his lifetime, Tony had never been *inside*. He had no idea what kind of hotel it was *now*, but he knew of its notorious (rumored) reputation in the not-too distant past. Supposedly it had contained the unofficial "offices" of the so-called Broadway mob. Meyer Lansky, Lucky Luciano, Bugsy Segal and Frank Costello turned themselves into multi-millionaires by conducting business within the Claridge's walls at 1500 Broadway. The business, none of which was legal, consisted of such things as counterfeiting (currency as well as passports), racketeering, gambling, extortion, prostitution, pornography, and more than a few murders here and there.

The streets of Manhattan were bustling now, with commuters eager to get home, theatergoers heading to their favorite restaurants, taxis honking their horns apparently just for the sake of it, and hookers on the lookout for an easy "john". Tony Dunlap knew better than to ever make eye contact with those wandering ladies of the evening although he had been approached often. His boyishly good looks seemed to be a magnet for them.

He *didn't* know what to expect, however, when he and Alistair Stickle would finally come face-to-face following his nearly seven-year disappearance. He was hoping for the best but fearing the worst. Entering the lobby on the 44th Street side, he looked around, trying to locate where the bar might be. A helpful bellhop pointed him in the right direction. The hotel was built in 1911 and he thought it was beginning to show its age. He expected the bar to be dingy, dimly-lit, probably dark wood-paneled, smelling of stale beer and decades of cigarette smoke, possibly with walls lined with old photographs of New York City and maybe photos of some celebrities (or mobsters and their molls) who had frequented the place.

The bar *was* dark. However the matte-black painted walls were adorned not by photographs but, instead, by expertly done copies of paintings by Jackson Pollock, Willem de Kooning, Franz Kline and Mark Rothko. Tony Dunlap stood with his mouth open at the sight. Definitely *not* what he was expecting at all. He failed to notice as the tall, extremely tanned blond man came up behind him.

"What do ghosts drink when they are thirsty?" whispered Alistair Stickle. It was an old joke from when they served together in that classified operation during the war.

Turning around slowly, Tony Dunlap answered "Ghoul-Aid."

The two men stood staring at each other for fifteen seconds before their hands clasped in the firmest of handshakes. Then they embraced.

"Don't say it, Tony," Alistair Stickle said as they slowly pulled apart. "It's way too cliché and it's not like you."

"Say what?" asked Tony Dunlap, shaking his head. "My god, you look fantastic, man! You're so damn tan. Have you been lying out in the sun naked for seven years?"

Alistair laughed.

"Let's sit, get a drink or five and all will be revealed. Well, all that I know of will be revealed. And thanks for avoiding the cliché, Tony."

"That being?"

"*Where the hell have you been all these years, you cowardly bastard, and why haven't you written?* Or something to that effect," snickered Al.

"I won't ask, Al. You have your reasons. I'll just assume that you sent those Christmas cards to let me know you were still alive. But there are, indeed, so many unanswered questions. I have a feeling I know what brought you *back* to the States, but I haven't a clue as to what drove you *away* from the States so quickly and mysteriously following your parents' murders," Tony said, looking his friend squarely in the face.

They sat at a small table in the corner of the room. The bar was slowly beginning to fill up with the early evening crowd. Commuters stopping in for a drink or two before heading home. Businessmen trying to close a deal. Theatergoers having a quick drink before the show. A portly cocktail waitress, obviously approaching retirement age, or possibly even several years beyond, sashayed up to them with a broad smile. She was wearing a shiny white silk blouse with a ruffled collar over wide-legged black silk trousers. She had flaming red hair, ruby-red lipstick, heavily rouged cheeks, and overly applied sapphire blue eye shadow. The effect was startling.

"What's your poison, boys?" she asked.

"Just for the fun of it," answered Alistair Stickle, "I'll have a Manhattan. Keep our tab running and then please charge it to my room."

Tony Dunlap stared at his friend once again.

MARC D. HASBROUCK

"I'll have a Vodka Martini," Tony said, still keeping his eye on his friend.

"Hmm," replied the waitress with her hand on her hip, staring at Tony's very tanned friend. "You struck me as the Tom Collins type. Who knew?"

Both men turned to look at the waitress. She shrugged her shoulders and headed toward the bartender.

The two men watched as she walked away.

"I wonder if she's Bozo the Clown's mother?" snickered Tony.

22

Veronica Barron, Billy Bennett, and Peyton Chase entered Sallie's Bella Luna Trattoria. It was fairly crowded with mostly teenagers and all of them talking and laughing at the same time.

"Yous guys back again?" Sallie shouted to them over the cacophony from behind the counter. "You flyboys just can't get enough of this high cuisine, can ya?" And he laughed raucously. "I see yous brought a gorgeous chaperone tonight. Gonna keep an eye on 'em, are ya, Veronica?"

"I'll try my best, Sallie, but you know what trouble makers these knuckleheads are," she laughed in return. "By the way, it's nice to be back."

Despite the crowd, the trio headed to their favorite and fortunately unoccupied booth by the window. Stella, Sallie's wife, brought them all glasses of water.

"Do you guys *really* need a menu?" she asked.

"Nah," answered Billy. "Ronnie and I are going to share a plain pie."

"And I'll have a calzone," interjected Peyton. "Have Sallie throw in some black olives with the rest of the junk in there, okay?"

"You got it!" answered Stella as she strolled away. "Cokes with that?" she called back over her shoulder.

"Beers would be better," answered Billy.

"You got it!" was the answer.

A perky teenaged girl skipped over to the jukebox, ponytail bouncing from side to side as she went. She dropped some coins in, made her selection, and skipped back to the table with her friends. Both Billy and Peyton rolled their eyes as the music began to play.

"Jesus," said Peyton, "is there any more insipid song on the planet than *Doggie in the Window?*"

"Oh," said Veronica, "I sort of agree with you, but I *do* like Patti Page."

Peyton snickered. "I'll go over and see if they have anything with the Andrews Sisters in that jukebox. *That'll* send the kids outta here in a flash."

Stella brought their beers and they all toasted to each other, taking big, long gulps.

"You know," began Veronica, "I was thinking this afternoon about the route that Alistair Stickle was…"

"Ronnie," interrupted Billy with a stern look on his face. "Please. No more of this murder shit, okay? I want you to get it totally out of your mind. We are *not* going to get involved. And I want you to totally concentrate on anything *other* than that."

Veronica looked him squarely in his face.

"What you want and what you're gonna get are two different things," she answered.

"Good god, you women are all alike," chuckled Peyton. "My mom said those exact same words when I asked for a BB gun for Christmas when I was six."

"Oh, yeah?" smirked Billy, "Peyton, I'm sure you heard those exact same words often when you were a horny teenager in high school."

Peyton gave him a friendly finger gesture.

"Boys, boys, boys," Veronica said, wagging *her* finger and looking around the restaurant. "Behave. We're amongst young folk tonight. Not that they even notice us old fogies."

Another older couple entered the restaurant. The distinguished if somewhat overweight man of around fifty escorted his female companion past the tables of loudly chatting teens.

"Hey, goombah," called out Sallie as he saw them enter. "And nice to see you, too, Annie. Yous guys been away too long. Sit, sit. I wanna have a tawk later."

The couple took a table at the far end of the restaurant. As far away as possible from the noisy teenagers. Stella took glasses of water to them and chatted quietly for a couple minutes.

"Regulars here?" Peyton asked Stella as she brought their meals. "I haven't noticed them before. Of course, Billy and I are usually here only for lunch."

"Fairly regular," Stella answered as she slid the pizza down in front of Billy and Veronica. "The Gallaghers haven't been in for a while, though. I guess he's been too busy with the murders."

Veronica's eyes lit up.

"Excuse me? What did you just say...or...what do you mean by murders?"

Billy gritted his teeth. Peyton rolled his eyes.

Stella nodded her head in the direction of that table at the far end of the room.

"That's Detective Lieutenant Gallagher and his wife Anne. He's on the Dover police force and he's been working in conjunction with his counterpart in Morristown and some other detective in Manhattan. It's about that horrible situation regarding Brenda Barratt."

"Oh?" said Veronica. "Oohh."

Tony Dunlap couldn't stop staring at his friend. It didn't go unnoticed by Alistair Stickle.

"Stop staring, Tony, you're making me uncomfortable."

"I'm sorry, Al, it's just...well, seven damn years. And nothing but a Christmas card every year. You don't think I was concerned? Confused?"

"You were just about to get married when I left, weren't you? And now you have kids."

"Yes, Al, and you were going to be my best man, remember that?"

There was an uncomfortable silence.

"Here ya go, boys," said the waitress as she delivered the drinks. "I'll need your room number if..."

"I'm paying," interrupted Tony. "It's on me tonight. And keep 'em coming. We might be here for a while."

And they were. Time just melted away. It was after 1 A.M. when they left the bar, and Alistair Stickle had told Tony Dunlap an earful.

It was after 1 A.M. when Veronica tiptoed quietly into the bedroom. She didn't turn on any light and was certain that Billy had long been asleep. She carefully undressed, pulled on her nightgown and slid beneath the covers feeling his warm body beside hers, his breathing barely audible.

The window next to the bed was open a few inches and she was lying there relaxing to the sound of the gentle spring rain that had begun to fall outside.

"If," Billy said suddenly and loudly, startling Veronica, "you're thinking for even one minute about contacting that police guy, Gallagher, I swear to God, Ronnie, I will surely smother you with this pillow!"

Silence for a beat.

"But you don't believe in God," she said.

"Then I won't have to atone for my sins," he said.

23

Following the announcement by the stewardess, Devon Stone buckled his seatbelt and secured his tray table in preparation for the landing at Idlewild Airport. The more he had thought about the almost-deadly explosion, the more he realized that he must tackle this situation head on and back where it originated. In the United States. In Manhattan. As much as he had *not* wanted to be involved in this murder, someone or something thwarted his intentions.

It was still early evening when he checked into the Algonquin and he thought, perhaps, that the nice, well-dressed detective, Lafferty, might still be at the precinct. He was.

"Detective Lafferty," said Devon as the officer came to the phone. "This is Devon Stone, young man, and I was hoping to never speak to you again."

The detective laughed.

"I was wondering," Lafferty said, "if perhaps your writer's curiosity would get the better of you sooner or later. May I assume that you're back in the States?"

"You may and I am. I'm at my old haunt, the Algonquin. I need to speak with you, preferably in person, as soon as possible. Care for a brew at my expense?"

"I'm officially off duty in thirty minutes. But I promised you the next drinks would be on *me*. And at Pete's Tavern. Grab a cab. All the New York cabbies know of that place. I'll meet you there in an hour, sir."

Forty-five minutes later Detective Lafferty slid into a booth, sitting across from Devon Stone who had arrived ten minutes earlier. Fastest cab ride Devon had ever had in Manhattan. Devon decided that he wouldn't make comment on the detective's attire, which, of course, was impeccable. But he had already started to formulate a future book in his mind with a dapper detective as a main character and with the temporary working title of *Dressed To Kill*. Even if he might now be a killer's target, Devon's creative mind was always working.

"You made excellent time, lad," chuckled Devon. "You must have had those sirens blaring to make it here so quickly. Great choice, by the way. This place fascinates me. I saw you come in and I just took the liberty of ordering you a frosty Schaefer, Lafferty."

The young waitress delivered the ordered drinks and coyly winked at Devon Stone as she set them down on the table.

"Your memory continues to astound me, sir," said Detective Lafferty as he lifted the frothy brew to his lips.

Devon ignored the remark as they toasted each other and he sipped from his gin and tonic.

"Have you made any headway in that heinous situation with Brenda Barratt?" asked Devon leaning back in the booth.

"Well, yes and no," answered the detective. "You mentioned at the time that the victim was expecting a guest for a late dinner the night she was murdered. So, with that information in hand, we questioned the desk clerks and bellmen at the Plaza. Apparently a lady and gentleman approached the check-in desk around eight that evening asking for Mrs. Barratt's room number. They were told that the desk couldn't give out that information for the sake of the guest's privacy, but the lady claimed to be Brenda Barratt's sister and wanted to surprise her on her first night back home in the States. The gentleman slipped the desk clerk a twenty and the room number was given. The desk clerk, by the way, has since been fired."

"Interesting," said Devon, leaning forward now, resting his elbows on the table. "I told you when you were in my room that following morning that Brenda must have known her assailant…or assailants…because evidently she opened her hotel room door so readily."

"Yes, sir, I do recall you saying that. But we had nothing else to go on at that time."

"But was it really her sister? I thought that her sister flew in from London several days later for Barratt's funeral."

"We checked with the airlines and customs at the airport. Her sister, Frances Wayne, did *not* enter the country until the day prior to Brenda Barratt's funeral. Evidently she had made all the funeral arrangements via long-distance. And spared no expense, at that. Based upon the description from the hotel clerk, the woman claiming to be the sister appeared to be a few years younger by at least a decade than Mrs. Wayne. By the way, Mr. Stone, why are *you* back in the States?

Devon smiled and signaled the bartender for a refill. For both of them.

"Before I answer that, Lafferty, did you get a description of the man who accompanied the pretend sister?"

James Lafferty gave a rather detailed description of the man in question at the Plaza Hotel on the night of the murder.

Devon Stone sat back in the booth once again, shaking his head.

"Hmmm. Well, well, well," he said. "That sounds very much like he just might have been the bloke who tried to blow me to kingdom come a couple days ago."

Devon Stone contacted his Manhattan-based publisher the morning after his arrival.

"Well, I'll be damned," gushed Bankston Bruin when he heard Devon's voice. "A nice and timely surprise, my friend! We've been trying to reach you. My girl's been calling you for the past two days. Don't you ever stay home? Where the hell are you, anyway?"

"I'm about ten blocks north of where you are at this very minute."

"What? What do you mean? You're back here in Manhattan?" asked an incredulous Bankston Bruin as he plopped down into his chair. "What brought you back here so soon?"

"To be brutally honest, I think I might be a target for a murderer and I want to bring this situation to a safe and healthy conclusion, for me anyway. Why were you trying to reach me so desperately?" asked Devon Stone. "Is something wrong? The book tours being cancelled or something?"

"Oh, Jesus, no!" laughed the publisher. "On the contrary. Your hand will fall off you'll be signing so damn many books from coast to coast. No, don't worry about that. This is a new one for us, Devon. Hasn't happened before so please be understanding with our American readers. There are a couple terms and incidents that you're using in your manuscript that leave our editors scratching their heads. I think these might be typically

Brit things but might leave our American readers confused. Would you be willing to do a minor rewrite here and there? Nothing too much, I promise. It won't affect the story in any way but might clarify some things for our audience here in the States."

Devon scrunched up his face, shaking his head, before answering.

"No problem," he lied. He hated having to cater to his American publisher in this manner, but if it sold a million copies, so be it.

"Great!" answered Bankston Bruin, clapping his hands together. "So, what's going on with this nasty murder business? I mean the *real* murder, not any that might be in your books."

Devon Stone relayed the story involving the note, *Memento Mori*, and the exploding package.

"Jesus Christ, Devon!" screeched Bruin. "Please let's get this thing solved before you get yourself killed. I'm expecting several more best-sellers out of you in the years ahead."

"Well, thanks for your concern about my safety," Devon said with more than a hint of sarcasm in his voice.

"Speaking about that murder situation, that female friend of yours… you know, that actress…has been here to see Tony Dunlap a couple times, I think. She seems intent on getting involved somehow. She better watch her pretty little ass, if you ask me."

Devon pondered that statement for a moment. *What is she up to now?* Devon thought.

"Thanks for letting me know that, Banks. I was hoping she and her boyfriend would keep their respective noses out of this. It could put them into serious trouble. Now that I'm back, I'll call them and admonish them as best I can."

There was a slight pause.

"I have no idea what other plans you might have, but now that you're here in the city, when can you come in, Devon? You know, those little rewrite things?"

Devon Stone glanced at his watch.

"I just had breakfast. It's going down to 10:30…I suppose I can be there within the hour. Will that do?"

"Hell, yes. Absolutely, Devon. I'll alert my editors. Holy cow, I was expecting that we would have to do this long-distance. Shouldn't take you too long, right?"

Devon shook his head again.

"Whatever you say, Banks, whatever you say."

Devon Stone arrived at Bruin Publishing at 11:15 A.M., ready for his "quick" rewrite.

Devon Stone did not leave Bruin Publishing until 6:55 P.M., his head in a tailspin. By changing a few "simple" expressions and incidents, he had to rewrite two complete chapters to make any sense for the American readers. He had never had to do this before in any of his previous books. *Was he being* too *British in his writing?* Devon thought, *or were the American readers becoming too dumb?*

Bankston Bruin offered to take Devon out to dinner and he readily accepted.

"Where do you want to go, Devon? You name it. And make it expensive. Bruin Publishing owes you."

"A couple years ago when I was here you took me to a great place a bit uptown from here called Gallaghers. Is it still around by any chance?"

"Ha!" laughed Bankston Bruin, "It's been around since 1927 and I can only assume that it'll still be going strong in 2027. Let's hail a cab."

"Let's not. I remember the size of those steaks," smiled Devon. "And it's a perfectly lovely evening, so let's work up an appetite and go by shanks' mare."

Bankston Bruin stared blankly at him.

"Hoof it. Stroll. Walk," said Devon as he smiled broadly and making walking motions with two of his fingers.

"I *know* what that means, Stone," smirked Bankston. "But I'm not as slim and trim as you are, dammit. And I'm definitely *not* a fan of exercise of any kind. I can't remember when I've walked further than three blocks here in the city. I'm serious."

"I'll carry you for the last few blocks if need be, old man," laughed Devon.

It was a beautiful spring evening when they stepped out of the Empire State Building onto 5th Avenue. Apparently countless hundreds of pedestrians were taking advantage of the perfect weather as well. The sidewalks were teeming. The two men slowly walked north, knowing exactly where they wanted to go. Twenty blocks later they turned west onto 52nd Street and walked two and a half more blocks, stopping in front of the venerable old Gallaghers Steakhouse. They could almost smell the sizzle. Bankston Bruin was sweating and stopped to catch his breath before they went inside.

"I may faint," wheezed Bankston as he reached for the door. "I need a drink."

Two hours later, having downed four gin and tonics, shared a $200.00 bottle of Barolo Riserva, and devoured the largest and the best roast prime rib of beef that he had had in ages, Devon stepped back outside while Bankston, also feeling no pain, paid the check and hit the restroom before emerging into the fresh night air.

"No more walking for the rest of the year, maybe even the decade," chuckled Bankston as he slowly stepped through the door. "I'm hailing cabs for us both. I've got to get down to Grand Central Station for my late train back home to Darien. I may hire a porter to carry me from the damn cab to the platform."

They both laughed and shook hands.

"Remember what I told you in there, Devon, about a possible suspect for the murders. Tony Dunlap has some interesting points to ponder. What he told me bears investigation. Wait. Why am I telling *you* to remember, for chrissake? You can't forget *anything!*"

A taxi pulled up to the curb and Devon opened the door for his publisher.

"Get home safely, old man," Devon said, with a mock salute to his friend. "We'll be in touch."

That cab drove off toward Grand Central Station downtown, and Devon summoned another taxi to take him safely back to the Algonquin. It was only a few blocks, but he was way too mellow to be stumbling around Manhattan. The cabbie took note of Devon's British accent and, thinking him perhaps a drunken tourist, made several unnecessary turns up and down streets that extended the ride a bit, bumping up the fare.

"Don't think I didn't know what you were doing on the way here, my good man," Devon chuckled, as the taxi pulled up to the hotel. "But don't worry. It's been a good night. I enjoyed the ride and I'll tip you well. Lucky for you I'm just about as drunk as a lord." And he giggled as he leaned forward to read the meter.

"Christ, you're expensive!" exclaimed Devon Stone.

The taxi's meter read $3.50.

Devon handed the cabbie a twenty-dollar bill.

"And keep the change. What there is of it!" he slurred.

Sleeping most of the following day, as much a result of too many drinks as well as the traveling hours finally catching up with him, Devon Stone had the hotel operator place a call to the home of his friends in New Jersey. He glanced at his watch and was horrified to realize that it was slightly after six in the evening. He had lost practically an entire day. But he *did* remember what Bankston Bruin had him told the night before about a possible murder suspect. He would keep that to himself until he could verify certain other things that his publisher had told him. He was intrigued but he had to admit that what he was told was a bit frightening.

Having answered the telephone while Veronica Barron was soaking in the bathtub, Billy Bennett was stunned to hear Devon's voice again and even more stunned to discover that Stone was back in the country. This situation was going in a direction he feared would not end well. But for whom?

Devon Stone told Billy about the exploding package, and recognizing the man who had tried to murder him as a fellow-passenger on the fateful flight on the night of Brenda Barratt's murder.

Billy sighed, closing his eyes and rubbed his forehead.

"Devon, Ronnie is going to be elated that you're back here, but where is this thing going?"

"Evidently your dear Veronica has been trying out for a new role. That of detective," answered Devon. "My American publisher told me quite a story last night and I think it's time we all get together and trade what we know and speculate about that which we do *not* know. What *is* going on, my friend, could fill two of my books. And probably will in time. Assuming, that is, I survive."

24

Alistair Stickle hesitated for only a moment before placing the call. There was a dire need to move as swiftly as possible. He was certain other murders might occur if he didn't intercede. But he was hindered by a couple of hard facts. Number one: he had re-entered the United States with a fake passport. Illegal. Number two: his driver's license had expired five years ago and he needed mobility.

"Miss Barron?" he asked as Veronica answered the phone.

"Yes?"

"I hope I'm not being too presumptuous. My good friend Tony Dunlap gave me your number. This is Alistair Stickle."

There was a slight pause and then Veronica Barron gasped, putting her hand to her mouth.

"Oh, my God!" she exclaimed. "What...I mean, why...seriously? Gosh, I mean, I can't believe I'm actually talking to you. You and your poor grandmother have been on my mind for days."

"I really don't want to get you involved in this situation...any more than perhaps you might be already, Miss Barron, but Tony told me about your strange, persistent interest. I'm a bit confused as to why."

"Don't worry about me getting involved, Mr. Stickle and, oh, please call me Veronica. I'm very intrigued by this mystery. I'd really like to help in any way that I can. My boyfriend will kill me...oh, damn...poor choice of words. I don't mean that in the literal sense, mind you! That sounded so callous, considering the situation at hand."

"Yes, I understand, Veronica," he chuckled. "Not really a laughing matter, but I certainly understand. And, please call me Al."

"Where are you? May I assume that you're back in the States now?"

"I am. And I'm staying at a hotel in Manhattan. Tony and I have had a very long conversation and that's how you came into the picture, Veronica.

I know that you and your friends are living out there in Dover. I need to see that painting. I need to do a lot more than that, but that's number one on my list. I checked into train schedules and I know the Lackawanna from Penn Station passes through Dover on a regular basis."

Veronica's heart began racing and her eyes widened.

"When do you want to come out here? Now?" she asked. "I'll meet you at the station. Today? Oh, my god…what time is it? I'll be there, just tell me when!"

"Whoa, whoa, whoa, Veronica," Alistair Stickle laughed. "Wait a minute. Slow down a bit. I didn't necessarily mean today. And I didn't necessarily mean for you to function as my taxi. Not yet, anyway. I have a couple other matters I must address first. I'll need to call the Preservation Society to alert them that I'll be there. I want to make sure someone will be there. Not sure yet if I'll use my *real* name or the one on my passport. And I'll want time to really examine that damn painting. All I'm asking of you right now is to be a conduit of sorts between the Dover police and me. It might put you in an awkward position considering that I'm not travelling legally. I'll be mindful regarding your safety. I hope."

"What do you mean by that…*you hope?*"

"Frankly…and I don't say this to alarm you in any way, Veronica… but I don't think the murders are over. I was a target once and I probably still am."

Now there was a very long, somewhat uncomfortable pause.

"Okay," Veronica finally said cautiously. "When you have your meeting with the Preservation Society, let's meet afterwards and have a long, private chat. My curiosity is working in overdrive at the moment. I won't mention this phone call to anyone…*especially* my boyfriend! But, and I repeat, I want to help in any way I can. Do you need the phone number for the Society?"

"Nope, thanks. Have it. I'm going to call there shortly and hope for the same discretion from them as I hope to get from you."

"You mentioned, Al, something about your passport a moment ago. You seemed to breeze right over it. Should I assume that a *fake* passport plays a role there?"

"You may, indeed, assume that. I am tossed about how to handle that situation with the authorities. There are severe penalties involved…

monetarily and prison-wise. Plus, I fled the scene of a murder several years ago, and..."

"Yes, I know about that, Al. Your friend Tony filled me in. But the police realize that you could not have committed that crime, so..."

"So...nevertheless I *still* fled the scene as well as the country. I've been missing and presumed dead for seven years. And now I suddenly show up amidst three other murders. Sounds suspicious, doesn't it? As far as anyone knows now, and according to my passport, I'm Benedict Tuttle."

"Maybe I should get my friend Devon Stone involved. He just got back into the States too and he could come up with a plausible scenario and solution, I'm sure."

There was a pause.

"*The* Devon Stone? The mystery writer who was chatting with my grandmother on the plane?"

"Exactly!"

"I had forgotten that Tony told me he was a friend of yours. That's interesting. Not that it matters, but I'm a huge fan of his. I've read all of his books. Very clever guy, for sure."

Veronica Barron began to speak again but was cut off.

"Hmm. Well, I'll get back to you, Veronica, after my trip to see *Memento Mori*. It's been some years since I've seen it."

"You didn't tell me where you are staying, Al. Which hotel are..."

But the call had ended.

~~~~~~

Alistair Stickle then had his hotel operator put through a call to the Dover Preservation Society. He introduced himself to the new director using his real name, which may or may not have been a huge mistake. He knew that he had to tread lightly and carefully. He was counting on the fact that perhaps, just perhaps, this lady had no idea about his past and his hasty disappearance.

"I need your assistance, ma'am, and discretion."

There was silence.

"How may I help you with that?" was the somewhat hesitant reply.

"I know you are fully aware of the nefarious doings lately regarding a particular painting. I would very much like to see it. And examine it.

But I need assurance that my presence will remain unannounced to the world. I fear for my life at the moment. As you probably know by now, I am one of the only two remaining heirs regarding *Memento Mori*. I have my suspicions but they will remain with me until an appropriate time. Will you honor my requests?"

Again, there was a long silence.

"And when would you like to come here, Mr. Stickle?" finally came the reply.

"How far are you located from the train station?"

"A five-minute walk. We're just a couple blocks up the street from it."

Alistair Stickle quickly glanced at the timetable he held in his hand.

"How does this afternoon around three sound to you?"

"I shall be here, Mr. Stickle."

And the call ended.

The train blew its loud whistle as it pulled away from the station. Alistair Stickle asked for directions to the Dover Preservation Society and was pointed in the right direction. He wondered, as he walked, if perhaps he had been foolish to give his true identity to the director. He could have been just an interested Dover citizen intrigued by the mystery. Too late now.

He walked up the hill, climbed the stairs to the front porch of the building and stepped in.

25

Alistair Stickle, accompanied by Alice Rose, the former assistant and now the newly appointed director of the Dover Preservation Society, carefully removed the painting, *Memento Mori*, from the wall. He had not seen it since he was a child but it was not as large as he had remembered it. Memories have a tendency to alter reality. The painting, including its old wooden frame, was 30" X 36" and was intimidating, to say the least. Dark and foreboding, the hooded skull of the Grim Reaper stared directly into the eyes of the viewer. The dismal color scheme of various shades of greys and black made the beady red eyes of the Reaper seem even more ominous.

"This painting gives me the heebie-jeebies," said the fidgety, nervous director as she stood next to Alistair. "Not because I know anything about old stuff like this, because I don't, but I don't know why anyone would want to have that awful thing hanging on their wall. I can't even look at it."

Alistair Stickle chuckled.

"I agree with you, Miss Rose, but for some reason my great-grandfather thought this was a real treasure. For some *strange* reason the artist's works, weird as they all are, have gained a lot of popularity throughout the years. For the life of me I can't figure out why this painting has been appraised for that outrageous amount."

Actually, he *did* know.

"I think the thing must be cursed," Alice Rose said, clutching her arms around herself and shuddering. "Your grandmother must have been killed because of it. The poor Langstons got killed because of it and now there isn't a lawyer in town that wants to handle this situation anymore. As far as I'm concerned, you can take it back. All of us on the board here at the society want it gone. We don't care about the money or the history of it."

Alistair Stickle felt sorry for the lady. Alice Rose was short, rail thin, looked frail and fragile – as if a strong gust of wind could easily lift her off the ground and carry her for several feet. Her salt and pepper hair belied the fact that she was probably only in her mid to late forties. Her hair was permed and set in the style of women much older than her, tight little ringlets close to her scalp. He thought, facetiously, that she must carry smelling salts in her purse because if anyone made a sudden jarring noise she would surely faint dead away.

He examined the painting closely then, turning it over, he examined the back. Carefully, he placed the painting face down on the floor and ran his fingers around the inside edges of the frame where it held the canvas. He leaned closer. He felt the backside of the painting, running his fingers across the old canvas. He turned the painting back around again and carefully ran his fingers across the surface of the painting. He leaned closer once again, so close his nose practically touched the surface. He propped the painting up against the wall and stood back staring at it, folding his arms across his chest.

"Hmm, interesting," he said almost to himself.

"What is it, Mr. Stickle?"

"I can't be positive, Miss Rose, but I don't believe that this is the original *Memento Mori*," said Alistair Stickle shaking his head. "No siree Bob. I think this is a forgery."

By the time Stickle reached the train station to head back into Manhattan, Alice Rose had placed a phone call.

26

"Don't show her!" Billy exclaimed slamming his hand down on the table after Peyton slid the newspaper article across to him. "If you value our friendship…and your life, for chrissake, please *do not* show Ronnie!"

They had been enjoying a regular, relaxing luncheon at Sallie's restaurant, having their usual meals when Peyton came across an article in the afternoon's Dover Advance. Billy skimmed through the article quickly about something that had happened at the Preservation Society the day before, but the headline was all he needed to know.

FAMILY MEMBER, ALISTAIR STICKLE, CLAIMS RETURNED PAINTING A FORGERY

"Ronnie hasn't mentioned anything about this case in days," Billy said with a look of alarm on his face. "I thought that I had convinced her to remain out of it. I repeated over and over again that we had no right to be involved. You remember what happened in London last year. That really wasn't her fault, but…it really *was* her fault. Sort of."

Peyton laughed. He knew what his friend meant.

"Isn't that Stickle guy the one who's been missing for the past few years?" asked Peyton between bites of his pasta.

"Yes," answered Billy closing his eyes and nodding his head. "The one with the Christmas cards from around the globe. Ronnie and I had the envelopes laid out in order of his travels. Son of a bitch. Obviously he's back in the States now. And, Jesus, he's obviously in…or around…Dover."

~~~

"Let the police handle it," Billy Bennett said as Veronica Barron held up the newspaper article. He and Peyton had just walked in the front door

131

from work and she was laying in wait. Peyton arched his eyebrows and made a hasty run for his bedroom.

She had been extremely surprised to see Alistair Stickle's name blasted on the front page. She thought he had been trying to remain under the radar, so to speak.

"But…" was all Veronica was able to get out.

"No buts," said Billy. "No, I take that back. Butt *out*! People have been killed regarding this situation. I do not want you to get us involved in any way. We had targets on our backs in London not too long ago. Remember that? Not fun, Ronnie. Not fun."

"All I was about to say, Billy, is that I could share some information with the police, that's all. What could *that* hurt? Maybe they already know what we know and then that would be the end of our involvement."

"*Our* involvement, Ronnie? *Our* involvement? I've tried my damnedest to remain out of it. You seem to keep including me. I've pleaded and pleaded with you. You took it upon yourself to go to New York and talk to that guy at Devon's publisher. You took it upon yourself to go to Brenda Barratt's funeral and piss off her poor grieving sister. Why can't you get this through your beautiful but exasperating head that it's quote- unquote none of our fucking business?"

"Can we at least go and have a look at that painting?" she asked. "I don't know why we haven't done that already. What harm would *that* do?"

"And that would put an end to your insane obsession about this case?"

There was a pause. Billy squinted at Veronica and cocked his head.

"Ronnie?"

"Probably," was her simple reply.

"Just you and me?"

"Well, Peyton can come too, if he'd like."

"Not interested!" Peyton called loudly from his room.

"When?" asked Billy with trepidation.

"Tomorrow…around seven in the evening."

Billy stood back, folding his arms across his chest, and glowered at Veronica.

"What. Have. You. Done?" he asked.

"Please don't get mad, Billy. We never argue but we've done a lot of that lately. I promise, just let's see the painting…out of idle curiosity…and be done with it, okay?"

"*Idle* curiosity? *Unfettered* curiosity would be more like it with you, frankly. You didn't answer my question, Veronica,"

"Oh, it's *Veronica* now," she answered.

"Still waiting."

"We have an appointment at the Preservation Society. It's usually not open at that time and I think we'll have a private showing," Veronica answered with a coy smile.

"You still haven't answered my question. Who is this appointment with? The new director of the place?"

"Oh, I'm sure she'll have to be there, you know, to unlock the place."

"Who else?" Billy was really getting more agitated as the questions flew by unanswered.

"Well," answered Veronica as she sat down on the sofa, twiddling her thumbs nervously. "I may as well tell you and wait for your screaming to stop. I made a couple phone calls this afternoon. I was a bit shocked after I read that newspaper article. The one, by the way, you were probably hoping that I *wouldn't* see. I know how you are. Anyway, I first called that guy at Devon's publisher. He got me in touch with Alistair Stickle. That's the guy that's been missing for seven years."

"Yes, I remember who he is, Ronnie. I shall try to remain calm. No screaming. Not out loud anyway. But I just said a very bad word in my mind."

"After he recently returned to this country, Alistair Stickle has been staying at a hotel in Manhattan. We had a couple of the *nicest* conversations. Believe it or not, he's read all of Devon Stone's books. He's a big fan. Oh, what an interesting person he is. He…"

"I don't care if he can walk on water, Ronnie. We'll meet with him. Look at the painting. And say 'goodbye, good luck, nice to meet you' and be gone. Right?"

"Of course, Billy, of course. Evidently, when he's finished with this nasty business here he'll be going back to where he's been living for the past year or so. Some island around Tahiti, I think. He's an artist too and, from what he tells me, he paints a lot of naked ladies."

"Count me in!" called Peyton from his room.

～

Veronica Barron, Billy Bennett, and Peyton Chase waited on the platform as the 6:50 from Manhattan pulled into the Dover station. Several commuters disembarked, walking to awaiting cars in the parking lot. Men in grey flannel suits carrying attaché cases, a few women in conservative dresses or business suits, and a couple men in casual attire, one carrying a large manila envelope.

Veronica spotted him right away, calling out to him as he looked around.

"You must be Veronica Barron," Alistair Stickle said with outstretched hand. "How did you spot me so quickly?"

They shook hands. Firm handshakes.

"Look around, Al," she responded shaking her head and rolling her eyes. "It's the month of May. This is northern New Jersey. You're the only one on the entire platform with a tan."

Veronica introduced Alistair Stickle first to Billy, and then to Peyton.

"Do you really paint naked ladies?" asked Peyton as he shook Stickle's hand.

Veronica shot him a look and swatted him on the shoulder.

"Idiot!" she laughed.

"Careful, Veronica, I might start answering to that if you keep calling me that," he said with a wink.

Alistair Stickle laughed out loud hearing the abrupt, brazen question.

"On occasion, Peyton," Stickle answered with a broad smile. "Just on occasion. I mainly paint big yellow lizards."

"Oh," was Peyton's simple reply.

"Come on, guys, it's only a couple blocks up that way," Veronica said pointing up the hill.

"Oh, I know where it is," said Alistair. "And I'm wondering what Alice Rose, the director, might have to say for herself after she totally betrayed my anonymity to the press."

27

It wasn't the Director who let them into the building. A very young gawky man sporting a crew cut and appearing to be in his early twenties greeted them.

"Miss Rose apologizes for not being here this evening," he said when he saw the look of confusion on Alistair Stickle's face. "She had a previous engagement that couldn't be broken. She called me and asked if I could be here tonight. I'm Jamie, and sometimes I help out here. I'm a student up at Centenary in Hackettstown. I'm majoring in U.S. history and this place truly fascinates me. I've heard all the hoo-hah over that ugly old painting but I don't know anything about it. I hope you weren't looking for any information about it, were you?"

"No, Jamie," answered Alistair Stickle. "I just want to show it to a couple of good friends. "I'll need to examine it along with them if you don't mind."

"Have at it, sir," the young man answered. "I'm studying for an exam, so I'll leave all of you in peace. Just let me know before you leave so I can lock up the place."

Jamie smiled politely as he left the room and walked to another part of the building.

Veronica waited until he had gone and was out of earshot.

"I thought you didn't want the world to know about you being here, Al," she whispered. "I was a bit shocked to see your name blasted across the papers a couple days ago."

"So was I, Veronica, so was I. Obviously Alice Rose was more interested in some more notoriety for the painting than my safety. I'm not surprised that she had, quote-unquote, a previous engagement. She probably didn't want to face me and be reprimanded. At first I thought I might have to go into hiding again. Maybe even flee the country again. I almost expected

135

the authorities to greet us here this evening. Surprised that they haven't. Maybe they have more pressing issues...or at least I can hope they do. For now. I'll have to face the truth sooner or later. And the ultimate consequences."

Billy and Peyton were getting restless and impatient.

"Can we just take a look at what this atrocity is and get the hell outta here?" asked Billy.

Veronica shot him a look. He returned it.

Alistair Stickle led them to the painting. He removed it from where it was hanging, placed the bottom edge on the floor and leaned it against the wall.

They all stared at it.

"Well, Ronnie" said Billy shaking his head. "I have to agree with that lady out at that cemetery. That *is* as ugly as a porcupine's asshole."

Peyton snickered. Veronica rolled her eyes.

"Don't pay any attention to these two blockheads, Al," she said.

"Who are you referring to?" asked Alistair. "What lady?"

"Oh," answered Veronica, "we attended your grandmother's funeral. It was her sister who said that."

"Hmm, my great-aunt," was the terse reply from Alistair Stickle. "You attended the funeral?"

He was silent for a beat. Frowning. Confused.

"Let's get back to the painting, shall we?" he finally said.

Alistair Stickle stepped away from the painting, shaking his head.

"This *was* expertly done," he said, "well enough to fool most people. I mean, the people who simply view this painting and not realize what the hell they are actually looking at. But I can almost guarantee who did it."

Veronica, Billy, and Peyton had no idea what he had seen or why he made that pronouncement.

"You're that certain it's a forgery?" Veronica asked.

"Oh, absolutely. As certain as sunrise. Without a doubt," Alistair replied. "Come closer. Look at the surface of the painting." They all leaned in closer to see what he was pointing at. "You see those fine little cracks in the surface?"

They all nodded.

"That's called craquelure. Many old…and I mean *very* old oil paintings will show that. It happens to the paint and varnish over time, as it ages. Now, obviously this painting isn't *centuries* old but it is still old enough to start showing its age like that. However, it's possible to artificially recreate the appearance of craquelure. But one must be careful in doing so because if it appears a bit too consistent it can be spotted by a true expert."

"But," asked Billy, "what makes you so sure this one has been faked? I mean, with all that cracked whatever you called it."

Alistair pulled a color photograph from the manila envelope he had brought with him.

"When I first saw the photograph of this painting in the newspaper article it made me wonder. Obviously it was a black and white photo, but I went to the newspaper and inquired about the photographer. Wonder of wonders…and bless his heart…he had photographed the painting long *before* it was stolen. And in color. He used Kodachrome film, which captures colors and intricate detail perfectly. I asked for a blowup of one section of the painting in particular, and in actual size."

He held the photo next to that same section in the painting in front of them. Veronica gasped. Billy and Peyton squinted.

"You see it, don't you?" Alistair asked.

"The cracks are different!" exclaimed Veronica.

"Exactly," answered Alistair Stickle. "Exactly. And the cracks on the painting we're now looking at are a little too uniform in appearance. The cracks produced by genuine craquelure are usually in irregular patterns."

"But what about the *back* of the painting?" asked Peyton. "You were examining that as well and you had a funny look on your face."

Alistair chuckled.

"The local experts, and I use that term loosely, around here who examined this forgery did a piss-poor job of it, if you ask me. Which of course, you just did. I believe the original painting was done around 1903. The back of the canvas should have darkened a bit with age by now."

He flipped the painting around so they could all see the back.

"Looks dark to me," said Billy. "Exactly how dark is it supposed to be? Couldn't canvas age differently?"

"Yes, of course. Very true," answered Alistair. "Conditions vary, obviously. Humidity, exposure to extremes in temperatures, what have you. The original has been hanging probably in the same spot in this old building for almost fifty years. So, really, I'm guessing as to what the back *should* look like. But the smart forger took no chances. He wasn't stupid, just careless, but he *thought* he took no chances. The back has been relined with artificially aged canvas. The textures and grain are not the same. And take another look. I assume that it's been taken down and cleaned from time to time. The *original* one, that is. Certainly in fifty-years time it *should* have been. Or maybe moved position. There should have been a *lot* of dust and probably more than a few cobwebs back there, too. It's way too clean for having been hanging there for nearly fifty years. I will give the forger his due, though. He dismantled and reassembled the old original frame expertly. He knew what he was doing."

"You keep saying *he*," said Veronica. "And you said you were certain you know who did it. So, who is your suspect?"

"He's my suspect regaining the *forgery*. I really haven't a clue as to who has been doing the killings. Or why. Could be him. Then again, maybe it's not," Alistair Stickle said, shrugging his shoulders.

"Well?" asked Veronica, hands on hips. "Who is it?"

"A ghost." answered Alistair Stickle.

28

"May I assume," Veronica began, "that by *ghost* you mean perhaps one of your counterparts in the war? In the Ghost Army?"

"Correct," answered Alistair Stickle. "I know that his grandfather was the painter of *Memento Mori*. The original painting. He and his grandfather were very close. And I remember that he was studying to be a painter as well. He certainly was a damn good illustrator, at least when we were over there in France pretending to be something we weren't. But there's another conundrum at play here. The painting has a rather murky provenance."

"You *are* speaking English, right?" asked Peyton, shaking his head. "I mean...conundrum. Provenance."

Alistair laughed and patted Peyton on the back. "You're priceless, man. Priceless. In English, then, there is still a major mystery or puzzle regarding not only when or why the painting was done, but also a record of the ownership of the damn piece of art before my great-grandfather got it. And how, exactly, *did* he get it to begin with. Did he buy it? Did he steal it? What were the conditions by which he put the painting on loan? And now, after all these years, what about it makes someone kill for it?"

But Alistair Stickle *did* know why. He just wasn't positive that he knew *who*.

~~~~~

Veronica's mind was racing a hundred miles an hour. She tensed up. Then she relaxed. Only to tense up again three minutes later. She definitely needed to contact Devon Stone. She waited until Billy and Peyton left for the gun shop early the next morning. She was so excited about the forged painting that she could barely speak when the call to Devon at his hotel room went through. The only problem was that she honestly didn't know *why* she was so excited about this information. Why would this change the scenario?

"Devon?" she blurted as soon as he answered.

"Yes, my dear Miss Barron," he chuckled, recognizing her distinctive voice. "It is I. Were you expecting someone else to answer?"

"You know, Devon," she responded, "you can be just as exasperating as Billy at times."

"I don't know if I should be honored or offended by that."

"Your choice, Devon, but please listen. I hope you're free because we'll drive in to the city later to pick you up. You *need* to see this painting. Grotesque doesn't describe it, but I'd love your take on it."

"But, Veronica, are we any closer to the reason for all the murders? Obviously someone must be afraid of what poor Brenda Barratt *may* have told me on that blasted airplane."

"Devon, my instinct tells me that Alistair Stickle knows more than he's letting on. Trust me, I can read people and he's holding something back."

Devon Stone thought about that for a brief second.

"He *was* out of the country when his grandmother was murdered, right?"

"Have we made a wrong assumption?" Veronica answered. "Could he actually be our well-tanned, cold-blooded killer after all?"

"Frankly, I doubt it, but can we now rule anything…or *anybody* out? Why was the original painting stolen, only to be quickly replaced by a forgery? Stickle seemed to call it a forgery rather quickly at that, didn't he? He's a painter, too, isn't he?"

Silence on both ends of the line.

"I'll call Billy at the shop and tell him the plan. Peyton can handle the place alone this afternoon. We'll pick you up at your hotel around one, okay? That'll get us out of the city long before rush hour. If you'd like, we can kick Peyton out of his room for the night and you can stay out here."

"No thanks, my dear. Considering the circumstances I'd feel much safer back in my hotel room tonight."

"Tell that to Brenda Barratt, Devon."

29

Billy was miffed when Veronica called him with her plan of action for the afternoon but, as always, he acquiesced. Veronica was eager for Devon to see the painting that caused so many murders, even if it was now considered a forgery. Traffic was light on the drive into Manhattan. They made great time. Devon was surprised when the front desk of the Algonquin notified him that he had a guest in the lobby. Billy had driven around the block so he didn't have to contend with parking the car. He was relieved when, after his third time around, he saw Veronica and Devon waiting by the curb.

It took them a bit over an hour for the drive back to Dover. Billy was lucky to find a parking space in front of the Society's building. All the cars parked along the normally empty street surprised him.

Peyton elected to head off to Sallie's Bella Luna Trattoria to wait for them when they were finished with their brief visit to the Dover Preservation Society. He hadn't cared for the painting the first time he saw it and didn't wish to refresh his memory.

Billy held the door open as Veronica entered, eager to hear what Devon's impression would be when he first sees *Memento Mori*. Surprisingly, the place was crowded. A dozen people milled around, staring up at the painting, forgery or not.

The three of them inched their way toward the painting and Devon stood, arms folded across his chest, as he stared at it.

"Creepy, huh?" said Veronica

"Ace," Devon said after a long silent pause.

"Excuse me?" asked Billy.

"I believe you Yanks might say brilliant," answered Devon. "As frightening and disturbing a subject matter that it might be, I believe it captures the title and meaning perfectly. Even if this *is* a forgery, I find it fascinating."

As he was viewing the painting, Devon stepped to the right. Then he stepped to the left and backed away a couple paces.

"Notice how the eyes follow you as you move?" he asked.

"Seriously?" Veronica was incredulous. "I think it's ghastly. Something that only someone like Dracula would hang on his wall."

They all chuckled at that.

Hearing their banter, Alice Rose, the Director, stepped from her office and smiled as she approached the trio. She stopped in her tracks, gasped, raising a hand to her mouth when she recognized Devon Stone. She took a couple steps backwards.

"It's...it's *you*," she uttered nervously staring at him. And he stared right back at her.

"Last time I looked it was me," said Devon, "or to be correct, it was I."

"You're Devon Stone," said Alice Rose, still staring. And Devon Stone was still staring back.

"Well, thank you for clearing that up, young lady. Frankly I wasn't sure who I was at the moment," snickered Devon.

"I...well...it seems," Alice Rose stammered, "I happen to be reading your very latest book right now! *The Fallen*. That is, I mean...I was reading it in my office when you all came in. What a coincidence. I'm flabbergasted! Could I get you to autograph it for me? Please?"

Devon winked at his companions and followed Alice back into her office as she retrieved the book, handing it to Devon.

"Do you have a pen, Miss...?"

"Oh, oh...yes, Mr. Stone, I do. And I'm Alice. Alice Rose. I'm a nervous wreck right now."

"I can tell," answered Devon, smiling, as he continued to stare into her eyes.

He took the book from her trembling hands and opened it to the title page. He continued to stare at her as he thought for a moment about what to write.

"Are you enjoying the book?" he asked with a smile.

"Oh...oh, yes, *very* much. Never in my wildest imagination would I ever expect to meet you, Mr. Stone. Much less to have you walk through these doors. In New Jersey, no less."

"I'm just full of surprises, Miss Rose," he answered as he began to inscribe the book.

He finished writing, closed the book and handed it back to her with a wide smile.

"My friends and I have a dinner waiting for us at a local establishment, Miss Rose, so we must not tarry. It was a very distinct pleasure, not only viewing this mysterious painting but meeting you as well. Perhaps we'll meet again."

He stood up, reaching out to shake her hand. She nervously held out hers. He felt that it was clammy and trembling slightly. A nervous Nellie.

"Enjoy your dinner, Mr. Stone," said Alice Rose as she slowly sat back down into her chair.

Alice Rose was still shaking. A nervous sweat broke out on her brow. She reached for the telephone as she opened the book that Devon Stone had just inscribed. After three rings, the call was answered.

"You'll never guess who's in town," she said with a smile.

She glanced down at the inscription.

Dearest Alice,
Revenge can be sweet!
Devon Stone
22/5/1953
P.S. Memento Mori

Veronica Barron, Billy Bennett, and Devon Stone walked down the front steps and then down the sidewalk heading to Billy's car.

"What is the name of the local detective who is working this case?" asked Devon.

Billy glared at Veronica. She glared back and shrugged her shoulders.

"It's Gallagher. Thomas Gallagher. And, no, Billy," she said turning to him with her hands on her hips, "I've been a good girl. I have *not* contacted him!"

'Well, then," said Devon Stone, "now might be the time to do so. Alice Rose was the person on my flight into Manhattan the night of Brenda

Barratt's murder. She was sitting next to the man who tried to blow my body to bits."

⁕

Peyton Chase was on his second beer by the time his friends arrived at the restaurant. He heard Billy chuckling with Devon Stone as they approached the table.

"So the detective on the case in Manhattan is Lafferty," Billy was saying, "and the guy out here is Gallagher. Gallagher and Lafferty. Sounds like a vaudeville comedy team, doesn't it?"

Both men laughed.

The trio joined Peyton at their favorite booth by the window.

"It's no laughing matter," scolded Veronica as they all took their seats. "Now I'm getting scared. One of the perpetrators is mere blocks away."

"We can certainly alert that Gallagher fellow," said Devon shrugging his shoulders, "but what could he possibly do? At this point, she has merely been seated next to a scoundrel on an airplane. But she's done nothing to warrant a call from the police. Gallagher hasn't even a reason to interrogate her. On what grounds? Hearsay?"

There was silence all around the table as Stella brought a couple menus for the group.

"*We* don't need them, Stella," said Peyton, "but our friend from the U.K. certainly does."

Devon Stone was introduced to Stella and, overhearing the introductions and seeing a new face, Sallie came out from the kitchen to introduce himself.

"I've heard your name bantered around by this unsavory group for a few months now," laughed Sallie, "I was hoping that sooner or later you'd partake of my exceptional cuisine on this side of the pond. No matter *what* these flyboys say about my cooking."

The two men shook hands as everyone laughed.

"Take a gander at the menu, Mr. Stone, these jerks know it by heart by now. If there's something that you *don't* see on it, just ask."

"Please, Sallie, call me Devon. Obviously I haven't had the chance to look at the menu yet, but I'll go out on a limb here. You wouldn't happen to make Fettuccine Cipolle e Pancetta, would you?"

Sallie clutched his chest like he was having a heart attack and took a step backwards. Stella, who was walking past the table with a tray of dirty dishes, stopped so abruptly the dishes nearly slid to the floor. Veronica, Billy, and Peyton looked at Sallie's reaction and their eyes widened.

"Are you shittin' me?" Sallie asked.

Devon Stone didn't know how to answer that question.

"Nobody. And I mean *nobody* has ever asked me for that dish in here before," said Sallie with the largest smile the trio had ever seen. "And you pronounced it perfectly. Nah, you won't see it on the menu but it's a dish that I make every Sunday night. At home. Just for Stella and the kids. My sweet mamma made it for me and my rowdy brothers when we was growing up. It takes a little longer to prepare it, that's why I don't have it on the menu. Most folks, when they come in here, if their pasta ain't swimming in tomato sauce it ain't Italian."

Devon sat back in his seat.

"You, my new friend," said Sallie, nodding his head, as he started to head back to the kitchen, "are in for a treat. It's on *me* tonight. *All* yous guys are getting this dish tonight. You'll be kissing Devon's feet before the night's over."

All three heads at the table turned to look at Devon Stone, their mouths still agape.

"Well," he said, shrugging his shoulders, "it never hurts to ask."

An hour later they were finishing their meals, complimenting Sallie and thanking Devon for the suggestion.

"That was, without exception," said Billy, patting his full stomach, "the best meal we have ever had here. Jeepers creepers, that was good."

They all agreed.

"I was so surprised to see all those people tonight there to see that wretched painting," said Veronica as she finished off her glass of wine, patting her lips with her napkin. "Even *more* surprising that now it's been called a forgery."

"You shouldn't have been surprised, Veronica," said Devon Stone. "Human nature and curiosity."

He paused for a moment.

"You know, back in 1911 the *Mona Lisa* was stolen from the Louvre in Paris," he said. "The painting was missing for two years. During those two years more people came to stare at the blank space on the wall where it had been hanging than had come the previous *twelve* years to gaze at the actual painting. That theft is what put the *Mona Lisa* on the map, so to speak. No one cared too much about it beforehand."

"How do you know that?" asked Veronica.

"He's a writer and he knows things," quipped Peyton.

Devon Stone winked at Veronica, nodded his head and shrugged his shoulders.

Veronica waited until Billy and Peyton had left for the gun shop the next morning. She dialed, and then asked for Thomas Gallagher when the telephone at the Dover Police Department was answered.

"Lt. Gallagher is due in any minute, miss," the receptionist said, "is there someone else who might assist you? May I ask what is the manner of your call? Is this an emergency?"

"No, that's alright," answered Veronica, "I'll just…"

"Oh, wait. Lt. Gallagher just came through the door," said the receptionist. "Give him a few minutes to get to his office and I'll put you through."

Veronica waited, drumming her fingers on the arm of the sofa.

"Gallagher," came the loud, sharp answer, startling Veronica out of her thoughts.

"Oh, good morning, sir," she replied. "You don't know me, but I may have some information that could help in your case regarding the murders of Brenda Barratt and those two others."

There was silence on the other end of the line.

"Are you still there, Mr. Gallagher?"

"Yes, I'm still here and it's *Lieutenant* Gallagher."

"Oh, well, I was wondering…"

"Let me stop you, miss, before you go any further. You're right. I *don't* know you. Jeez, I don't know if it's all because of that god-awful painting, the full moon, superstitious religious zealots, or just a bunch of crackpots released from the loony bin all at once, but I've been getting so-called tips about this murder for days now. The painting is cursed. The devil himself did it. It's a commie plot. End times are approaching…and on, and on, and on. So unless you can give me some rational, concrete information I'll say have a good day and go play with your cat, your dog, yourself, or whatever."

Veronica was, at first, embarrassed and then steaming mad. *The nerve of that guy!* But she composed herself quickly, introduced herself and calmly began her story.

"I wasn't aware, sir, of the prank calls you may have been getting. But please listen to what I have to say. I'll be glad to come to the station if you want, but I'm *not* a crazy person. The truth is, though, you might not be able to act on what I tell you. You might consider it hearsay, but I think you'll be able to verify some of the facts."

A brief pause.

"Go on," Gallagher replied reluctantly.

Veronica went to great lengths to tell the complete story. Devon Stone's flight from London, the brief conversation with Brenda Barratt, the two people he recognized as being on that flight, his escape from an explosive device, and ending with the trip to the Preservation Society where Devon recognized Alice Rose. She avoided mentioning Alistair Stickle, not wanting to draw attention to the fact that she knew of his being back in the country. Although, she knew that Alice Rose certainly had mentioned it to the press.

"Okay, Miss Barron, you have me intrigued. Yes, I heard about Stone from Detective Lafferty in Manhattan. But how do we know that Stone's memory is reliable?"

"Don't ask me how, Lieutenant, but if you happen to have a conversation with Devon Stone this afternoon, he'll be able to quote you word-for-word a year from now. Trust me!"

Veronica heard a long loud sigh from the other end of the line.

"And how, exactly, do *you* fit in to all this, Miss Barron? Are you related to the deceased? Frankly, I don't understand your involvement."

"I'm a good friend of Devon Stone, *Lieutenant* Gallagher. I'm concerned for his safety and I simply want to help."

"That sounds nice, Miss Barron," Gallagher said with just a hint of sarcasm. "But you said that you and a couple of your friends were at the Preservation Society when this Stone guy recognized Alice Rose. Isn't it just possible that *she* recognized *him* as well? And I don't mean as a famous author, but as someone who can put the finger on her. Stone might now have yet *another* target on his back, don't you think? For that matter, you and your friends might not be outta the woods either. Did you ever think about *that* before getting yourself involved?"

"We've all been in tight situations before, Lieutenant, but there's no need for me to go any further with that one."

Gallagher vacillated between his next move and what Veronica Barron had told him.

"Well, I can go see Alice Rose, Miss Barron, but I have to tread lightly there. I have no reason to believe, aside from your words, that she has anything to do with the murders. You *do* understand that, don't you?"

"Yes, sir, I do. I've told you all I know and we'll just have to let it play out, I guess."

But Veronica Barron had *not* told him everything she knew. Veronica only hoped that, if Gallagher questions her, Alice Rose doesn't mention that she, Billy Bennett, and Peyton Chase were with Alistair Stickle while they were studying the forged painting.

30

Alice Rose, more nervous than ever, wished that she had kept the front door to the Dover Preservation Society locked tight when she first arrived. But she hadn't. Not that it would have made any difference, honestly. That was the first mistake of the day. She was about to commit the second mistake, a mistake she would soon regret.

After introducing himself, Lieutenant Thomas Gallagher sat down in the uncomfortable old wooden chair across from Alice's desk in her office. He didn't really know how far he could or *should* go without probable cause, but perhaps he could rattle a cage or two.

She had thought, at first, that he might have been with the press. Until, of course, he introduced himself. To avoid fidgeting, she sat on both of her hands, hoping that he wouldn't notice.

"So, tell me Miss Rose," began Gallagher with a friendly smile, "did you enjoy your recent visit to London?"

The question threw her for a loop. She wasn't expecting *that* one at all.

"Oh," she answered with a confused look on her face. "I thought you were going to ask about that wretched painting."

She pointed to *Memento Mori*, which was hanging on the wall across from her open office doorway. Gallagher turned and glanced at it quickly.

"We shall get around to that, don't worry, Miss Rose."

"I...don't...well..." her stammering caused Gallagher to sit back in the office chair, casually crossing his legs as he stared at her.

"Do I make you nervous for some reason?" asked Gallagher, staring at her without blinking. "I believe my question was a fairly easy one."

Lieutenant Thomas Gallagher was known to have an almost hypnotic way of interrogating people. His voice was deep and soothing, easily putting his subject at ease. He often held a stare without blinking for several minutes. It was rumored back at the precinct that suspects might even confess to things they hadn't actually done because of it. But that was just a rumor.

Alice Rose collected her thoughts.

"Should I have a lawyer present for this questioning?" she asked abruptly.

"Is my asking about a recent vacation trip to London one that might require legal assistance or counsel?"

"Well…no, I suppose not," was the meek reply. *But how did he even know about my trip?* she thought.

"My wife and I have travelled to London often, Miss Rose. Wonderful city. One of our favorites. Have you ever stayed at the Plaza Hotel in Manhattan?"

Another question out of the blue and caused Alice Rose to blink repeatedly.

"What? Oh, my heavens…no. Never," answered a now quivering Alice Rose. "It's *far* too expensive for my meager budget. And I'd…"

"And yet you flew first-class from London. Hmmmm."

Matteo Amato had parked his car on the street in front of the Dover Preservation Society and was about to open his car door when he saw the detective walk up the front steps and enter the building. Amato knew who Lieutenant Gallagher was. He had an encounter or two with him in the not-too-distant past regarding some minor misdeeds, but had managed to lie so convincingly that he was sent on his way. Matteo Amato was cunning and shrewd but not the most intuitive soul on Earth. Gallagher knew the man was lying but let him go to watch him swing in the breeze for a while. They were minor infractions, but ones to keep Matteo Amato on Gallagher's radar.

Amato, slinking down in his car seat as much as possible to avoid being seen, would wait until Gallagher left.

Half a block away, on the opposite side of the wide, oak-lined street, another car sat parked. Unnoticed. Another pair of eyes watched the building, glancing back and forth to the car containing Matteo Amato.

"What is the Society's decision regarding that painting?" asked Gallagher as he turned and pointed to *Memento Mori*. "I understand, now, according to Alistair Stickle, one of the heirs, that it might be a forgery. I read it in the newspapers. Is that true?"

"Mr. Gallagher…or do I call you Detective Gallagher?"

"*Lieutenant* Gallagher will be fine, Miss Rose."

Alice Rose removed one of her hands from beneath her thighs and waved it toward the painting.

"We want rid of that horrid thing," she replied. "Gone. Out of our sights."

"Are you at liberty to discuss the original conditions upon which the painting had been placed on loan to begin with, Miss Rose?"

There was a long, uncomfortable pause.

"Perhaps I *do* need a lawyer present," answered Alice Rose as she stood up.

"Perhaps you do, Miss Rose. Perhaps, then, you do."

Lieutenant Thomas Gallagher stood up as well, and turned toward the door.

"Let's meet back here again tomorrow, Tuesday morning at ten. Legal counsel present."

"Oh, no, that won't do, Lieutenant Gallagher. Definitely not. Tomorrow is impossible. The Society hasn't found a new lawyer yet. There isn't a lawyer in town that wants anything to do with this case or that painting. They all seem to be afraid for some reason. But I've been in discussion with a couple of them over in Whippany. They might be interested but it will take time. Please give me a week or so, alright?"

He pondered this for a moment or two, placing his hands on his hips and staring intently and unblinking into her eyes. *She's obviously stalling*, he thought. He took a deep sigh.

"Very well, Miss Rose. I shall wait for your call, but if I don't hear from you in one week I'll be back. May I also suggest that you be very careful? I believe that this situation just may turn nasty before it reaches a conclusion. But, that's just a suggestion. Good day, Miss Rose."

He handed her his business card, glanced at the painting one more time and, with that, Lieutenant Thomas Gallagher was gone.

Alice Rose turned to look out the window that was behind her desk, clenching and unclenching her fists as she did so. She felt like screaming. Or fainting. Or running away.

Five minutes later she heard the front door to the building open and footsteps on the hardwood floors. She wanted to hide under her desk. Or to be suddenly in Alaska.

"What did that nosy flatfoot want?" Matteo Amato asked loudly, making Alice Rose jump and let out a tiny scream.

Silence.

"Well?"

"He knows about my flight from London. And he knew I flew first-class. I have a feeling he may have heard about it from Devon Stone. The writer was here to see the painting. Along with his two friends who live here in Dover."

"What else? Surely he wasn't here to discuss London, was he?"

"I don't know. He's not finished. He wants to talk about the original deal regarding the painting. I'm sure he must have put two and two together. I don't know if he knows anything about Frances Wayne, but he's not dumb. He'll be back next week and he wants me to have a lawyer present."

"You're an idiot. And a nervous Nellie. He'll have you behind bars before you can say Jack Robinson," Matteo Amato growled.

"I never should have gotten involved," sobbed Alice Rose. "If I knew people were going to die because of all this nonsense I would have walked away. This has gotten way out of control. But..."

"But, you *are* involved, you dumb broad," sneered Amato. "You're an accessory after the fact, as a matter of fact. Just as guilty as if *you* had sliced Barratt's throat."

Deathly silence as they each stared at each other.

She thought about her next statement, took a deep breath, and tried to regain her composure. "But I'll play coy. You'll see. I'll give him details about the contract that was signed fifty years ago and no more. I promise."

Amato wasn't so sure.

"Why not come back tomorrow? Why is he waiting until next week?"

"Oh, he wanted to, but I told him the Society doesn't have a new lawyer yet. That's true, right?"

"What the hell are you talking about? I thought those yokels over in Mine Hill agreed to take the case on?"

Alice Rose thought she just might faint.

"It's Whippany and, yes, they sort of agreed. The rest of the board hasn't approved anything yet. But the cop doesn't know that."

"I repeat. You're an idiot. I can't do too much to the cop for now, but that Devon Stone creep is cruisin' for a bruisin'. I fucked up once but not this time. His pals are due for a visit from the Grim Reaper and I sure as hell don't mean that painting."

"What are you going to do?"

"Never mind. The less you know, the less you can squeal like a pig to the cops."

Matteo Amato turned on his heels and stormed out of the building, slamming the door as he left.

His exit was so noted by a pair of eyes half a block away. On the opposite side of the street. In an unnoticed parked car.

31

Alice Rose fretted about her upcoming meeting with the detective. She wasn't sure what he might already know. He had cautioned her, but was he simply trying to frighten her into some form of confession?

Following her unsettling discussion with Matteo Amato earlier in the day, she began to be concerned about her own safety. Although she had hardly ever used it, she kept a small pistol, loaded, in her bedroom night table drawer. It was a .25 caliber FN Baby Browning.

Matteo Amato decided that he couldn't take any more chances. Loose ends definitely needed to be taken care of. And now Alice Rose was a *very* loose end. She might remain silent and not divulge anything damaging to the authorities. But then, she was a nervous biddy and might spell out the entire scenario to save her own neck. He knew where she lived. In a little, modest house on a quiet street in Mine Hill, less than two miles from where she worked. He was cautious. He could dispatch her quickly, unobtrusively and no one would be the wiser. He felt as though he had been extremely cautious regarding his activities within the past week or so. No one but Alice Rose knew that he was even back in the States.

But he was mistaken.

After locking up the Preservation Society for the day, Alice Rose made a hasty run to the A&P to pick up some cookies and a nice tea to sip while watching a bit of television and a few of her favorite shows, especially *I Love Lucy*. It would take her mind off the horrible situation, at least for a couple hours or so. Lieutenant Gallagher and Matteo Amato had rattled her nerves. She pulled her car into her attached garage, hurrying into her house as quickly as she could, shutting and locking her front door. Matteo Amato stepped carefully from behind a row of tall hedges that separated her house from the large wooded expanse of property next door, looking up and down the street to make certain he hadn't been seen.

But he had been seen. From a safe distance.

Alice Rose turned on the television and put a kettle on the range to boil for a cup of tea. *Teatime with Lucy* chuckled Alice. She would call the lawyers in the morning to get this nightmare over. Maybe no one would be the wiser. Suddenly there was a soft knocking on the front door. She jumped, letting out a gasp. Before going to the door to look through the peephole, and just to play safe, she ran to her bedroom and hastily got her pistol, holding it out in front of her. She gasped again when she saw who was at the door, putting the little pistol into her apron pocket.

"Alice," whispered Matteo Amato, "I know you're in there. Let me in. I just want to talk. It will take only a minute and then I'll be gone. Promise."

"Are you mad at me?" asked Alice Rose. "We didn't leave on such a friendly note this afternoon."

"Oh, don't be foolish," answered the man, as he slowly withdrew a serrated knife from his jacket. He held it behind his back as he heard the door being unlocked. *Foolish, foolish woman*, he thought.

"How could I be mad at *you*, Alice? We're in this thing together. We're partners."

He snickered.

"Why are you here?" asked Alice Rose nervously as he stepped into the room. "You certainly didn't come here simply to apologize, did you?"

"We have some loose ends to tie up," answered Matteo Amato, stepping a bit closer, leaving the door behind him open for a quick getaway. "And you know how I *hate* those loose ends."

As he made a slow move toward Alice, he brought the knife around so she could see it. Alice Rose stepped backwards and gasped again.

"Loose ends need to be cut, don't they, you silly old bitch?" he chuckled. "I can't trust you to keep your yap shut."

"You...you can't be serious," Alice Rose said as she eyed the knife. "I told you I wouldn't say anything I shouldn't. I promise. Put that horrible knife away. I'll shoot you first. You're scaring me!"

She pulled her little pistol from her apron pocket, holding it with both hands and frantically waving it in front of him.

Matteo Amato nearly doubled over in laughter.

"Well now, ain't that cute," he said with a smirk. "What the hell is *that*, a frickin' water pistol? You'll make me piss my pants from laughing, you scrawny old maid!"

Alice Rose backed up again, still waving the gun. Matteo Amato tossed the knife at her feet. That action confused her and, foolishly, she looked down at it.

It was his opportunity.

He lunged forward, grabbing the hand that held the pistol. He forcefully pushed her backwards and she fell, with him on top, onto the floor.

"You are *so* stupid," he hissed into her ear as she began to cry and fight back. But he was too strong and she could hardly move. He wrested the gun from her hand and immediately thrust the short barrel into her mouth. His thumb slid the safety lock open. Eyes wide in abject terror, her muffled, frantic cry was drowned out by the gunshot and by the whistling teakettle in the kitchen.

Matteo Amato stood up, reaching over to pick up his knife before the spreading pool of blood could get to it. After carefully wiping it clean with his handkerchief, he put the pistol in the dead woman's hand. He thought that making it look like a suicide was a stroke of genius.

But *he* was the stupid one. And not very observant.

32

Lieutenant Gallagher shook his head as he wrote up the police report. Several aspects about the death of Alice Rose bothered him.

Why would anyone put on a teakettle to boil and then blow her brains out? After the water had boiled away, it was the acrid burning aroma of the teakettle and the ensuing smoke that had drifted out the open front door of the house that had drawn the attention of someone who obviously was nearby, who then alerted the fire department who then, in turn, alerted the police.

Why would anyone lie down on the floor to blow his or her brains out? The blood splatter pattern, skull fragments, and brain matter on the living room carpet along with the pooling blood under her body attested to that point.

And, most tellingly, why would a left-handed person shoot her brains out by holding the gun in her right hand?

33

Early springtime…1903
On the West Side of Manhattan

The driver had not wanted to turn northbound onto 11th Avenue but by being in the wrong lane he was forced to. Traffic was heavy and he simply could not maneuver his new little car out of the flow. The amount of traffic of all kinds suddenly made him nervous. Horse carts, cars, trucks, throngs of people surrounded his car and, startlingly, a slowly moving on-coming steam engine was heading straight toward him. He was in the middle of railroad tracks. Two men on horseback rode in front of the steam engine waving red flags while other vehicles and the pedestrians scattered out of the way. The driver managed to get his car off the tracks and out of harm's way, but just barely.

A young mother and her little boy were among the pedestrians vying for space on the avenue. She was shopping for the fresh vegetables that trucks were bringing into the city from the surrounding farmlands to the west of the island. Her son, a rambunctious four-year-old, was getting bored and more difficult to keep by her side. The mother clutched his hand tightly as they waited for some traffic to ease enough allowing them to cross the dangerous street. A horse whinnied loudly on the opposite side of the busy avenue and the boy's ears pricked up. He saw the horse and wanted to pet it. He suddenly broke free from his mother's grasp and ran into the street.

From the corner of his eye, the driver saw the young boy but it was too late. Although his car wasn't going that fast, he applied his brakes as quickly as he could but to no avail. He felt the awful thump and his heart nearly leaped out his chest. He saw a young woman rushing up to the side of his car and watched as she crumpled to the ground.

Her anguished scream was almost drowned out by the shrill whistle from the passing train.

34

Present Day

Veronica Barron sat across the table from Devon Stone in his hotel suite. Devon had managed to get an auction brochure from Sotheby's. They examined the brochure showing photos of the paintings done by the late Matteo Amato decades before. Neither Billy Bennett nor Peyton Chase wanted anything to do with this situation, so they had remained at home.

"These paintings are more than bizarre," said Veronica, scrunching up her face. "They are morbid and frightening. Dead animals. Dead flowers. Vultures picking at a carcass. Why the heck would anyone even consider buying them?"

"Granted, these are grotesque, my dear, but art doesn't always have to be pretty. There are a couple famous pieces that immediately come to mind that I find chilling. Late in life Goya painted an unsettling one called *Saturn Devouring His Son*. Gory and grotesque. Van Gogh painted one, *Skull Of A Skeleton With Burning Cigarette*, which leaves me bewildered, for example. I actually own a painting by Frida Kahlo. She often addresses such dark themes as death and suffering. And look at *all* the artwork about a dying Christ on the cross. Pious perhaps, but certainly not what I'd call pleasant. There are countless pieces of artwork done through the ages that deal with death and dying. Not all artwork must have beautiful flowers and pastoral landscapes and faces of happy children playing in the surf. Some of *that* kind of stuff makes me gag."

"So says the murder writer!" laughed Veronica.

"No, I think we might be looking at something deeper here, Veronica," answered Devon Stone. "I think we are looking at a form of history. This one here really intrigues me," he said as he pointed to one of the photos. "This might have set the whole weird recent murder scenario going. According to the information here in the brochure it appears to have been painted the same year as *Memento Mori*, doesn't it? Bloody hell, I think this one confirms something that my publisher told me."

The painting in question was titled *Avenue of Death, NYC*. It depicted an anguished woman, possibly the mother, clutching an obviously dead child to her breasts as she sat straddling railroad tracks, with cars and city buildings around her. She appeared to be wailing in despair. The color palette, as in most of Amato's works, was dark. Tones of dusty greys and murky browns. Even the sky, what could be seen of it, was grey and forlorn.

"This other one," said Veronica as she examined one more photo, "seems so incongruous, doesn't it?"

It was titled *West Side Cowboys*, and it was a painting with the viewpoint looking straight down a very crowded city street lined with railroad tracks. But coming right toward the viewer were two men in western gear astride horses. Close behind them was a large, foreboding steam engine. The viewpoint was as if the artist was sitting on the ground and the subject matter seemed to tower over him. The only bright color in the entire painting was the deep blood red of the flags on poles that the men were carrying in their hands.

"I think we might need to do a little research at the library for what these might mean," suggested Devon Stone. "That title, *Avenue of Death*, obviously refers to something that affected the artist, Matteo Amato, to a great degree. Poor Brenda Barratt may have been right about subject matter for one of my future books. This plot gets far more intriguing the further it goes. And far more sinister."

35

As much as she didn't like to be, Frances Wayne was back in the United States. She hoped it would be for a short time. As short as possible. Being that she had to close out the estate legally, she figured she might as well stay at her late sister's apartment. It certainly was convenient. And she could play the grieving sister to the hilt. She wasn't certain, but she had assumed that she was the sole surviving member of her family following her sister's murder and that the entire estate would come to her. She wasn't aware of a will or a reason that would prove otherwise even though she and Brenda Barratt had not been on the best of terms for decades. For that matter, they actually hated each other. Her sister's last visit in London had not improved the situation any. In fact, it had ended in anger, tears and very harsh words. Could that last visit be something that she had discussed briefly with Devon Stone on the airplane? She doubted it, but there was no way at all of knowing that now. And then her plan had suffered a major bump in the road. It was quite unsettling to discover that her great-nephew, Alistair Stickle, was not only alive but now within a few miles. He needed to be dealt with quickly, meaning that he must be dispatched. And as discretely as possible. Making it appear to be a horrible accident. But could she now completely rely on Matteo Amato? He was ruthless and certainly cold-blooded. True, he had mistakenly killed Stickle's parents years ago and gotten away with it. Although, in the long run, that had worked out for the best. They needed to be taken out of the picture sooner or later. He had just gotten to them sooner. True, he had swiftly and deftly taken care of the lawyer and his sister at the Preservation Society. They each knew too much and could have been major liabilities. Although it pained her greatly, she was relieved that he and Alice Rose had killed her annoying sister. Years of rancorous sibling rivalry ended swiftly that night. But he failed miserably when it came to that obnoxious and way too clever author,

Devon Stone. The conversations within the past couple days with Matteo had unnerved her. Perhaps she had been a bit too cavalier regarding her conniving friendship with Amato over the years. That fact was slowly beginning to dawn on her.

~

Matteo Amato had thought their plan had been infallible right from the very beginning. Frances Wayne had actually been the one to approach *him* years ago with the devious plot. But it appeared to be unraveling quickly and he hated loose ends. He hadn't liked the way their recent conversations had ended.

Devon Stone was *still* a major loose end. What did he know? What did Brenda Barratt tell him on that airplane? His first attempt to kill him did not work out well.

That pretty little actress was a loose end. She was a nosey bitch. Why was she asking so many questions? Too many questions. And what did she already know? Could she have figured out what had been going on and alert the media...or the authorities?

Her boyfriend fell into that loose end category by default. But, what the hell? He needed to go, too.

And what if Frances Wayne really *didn't* follow through with their original plan? What if she ended up double-crossing him? Another loose end?

His mind was racing and his temper was rising.

36

Veronica Barron made an astute assumption that Frances Wayne just might be staying at her deceased sister's apartment in Morristown. It was an assumption that she would soon regret.

Perhaps the sister might be more amenable to meeting again, now that Veronica felt she had some pertinent information to share. As far as Veronica knew, Frances Wayne could still be a target for whoever is doing the killings regarding that ugly painting. She had no idea if Frances Wayne was even aware that her great-nephew, Alistair Stickle, was back in the States. Back from the dead, as it were. It was the *incorrect* assumption of Frances Wayne's imminent danger from whoever was doing the killings that proved problematic.

Billy Bennett was extremely hesitant to try for another meeting with Frances Wayne. He was still stinging from the icy stare and harsh words from that day in the cemetery. Reluctantly he had driven Veronica to Morristown. They were able to find Brenda Barratt's address in the telephone directory, but the telephone simply rang unanswered when Veronica attempted to call. It was a long shot to even hope to find Frances Wayne there but Veronica felt it was at least worth a try. Perhaps someone else there might know where she might be.

The apartment building, when they found it, was a five-story mastery of simple, clean modern architecture. Set back from the street, it was fronted by a parking lot, a perfectly manicured lawn and small garden areas. Although basically an unassuming box-shape, the first two floors of the exterior were a pale grey stone, with the remaining three top floors a crisp white stone. All of the narrow vertical windows were set within stark black frames. It would have been considered austere had it not been for the neatly trimmed greenery surrounding the base, punctuated on either side of the entryway by tall, slender Italian Cypress.

Billy parked the car in the visitor's parking area.

"Are you sure you want to do this?" he asked.

Veronica took a deep breath and opened her car door.

"Let's go," she responded. "Perhaps she has gotten over the horrible shock of her sister's murder and might be in a friendlier mood. Who knows?"

"Who knows? She might beat us to death with her broomstick," Billy answered.

Veronica rolled her eyes.

When they entered the front door and walked down a short hallway lined with mailboxes into the main part of the ground floor their mouths dropped. Their eyes immediately shot up toward the ceiling. A large square stained glass skylight topped a huge atrium that extended up the entire five floors. The lobby floor was a stark white marble with soft veins of pale grey running through it.

They could tell, as they looked up, that the various apartments themselves were situated around the square shape of the atrium. An elegant black wrought iron railing surrounded each landing, separating the atrium from the hallways in front of each of the apartments. There was one elevator on each of the four sides of the lobby, as well as an enclosed stairwell.

Veronica checked the directory at the main entry and found the late Brenda Barratt's apartment number. 310. There was a call-button and speaker next to the apartment number but Veronica ignored it.

She grabbed Billy's arm and led him to the elevator.

"Be prepared to run, Ronnie," he said as he reluctantly got into the elevator.

It was slow and dinged quietly as the doors opened onto the third floor. Apartment 310 was just past the entry to the stairwell.

"Nothing ventured, nothing gained," said Veronica with false bravado.

"Cliché, Ronnie, not up to your standard. You need a better scriptwriter."

She stuck out her tongue at him.

They knocked on the door lightly. Nothing. Then a bit harder. Nothing. There didn't appear to be a doorbell. They waited a minute more and knocked once more. They heard an elevator softly ding. Billy turned, looking around. He walked over to the railing. One floor below, on the opposite side of the atrium an older couple emerged from their elevator and slowly walked to their apartment. The elderly man looked up and, seeing Billy, gave a friendly wave of his hand. Billy waved back. Unlocking their door, the couple disappeared inside.

"We're safe, Ronnie, nobody's here...come on, let's go!"

Veronica hesitated but finally stepped back from the door.

"Okay," she said with a sigh. "You're right, Billy, but she's been here. Recently. I can tell. Can't you smell it? I'm picking up a *very* faint whiff of Shalimar. Oh, well. I'll try calling again later."

"Come on. I'll race you down the stairs, Ronnie. That elevator is too slow for my tastes. And I'll race you to the car."

Just as they entered the stairwell, with the door swinging closed behind them, the elevator dinged on the third floor.

Frances Wayne and Matteo Amato stepped out onto the third floor landing carrying grocery bags and headed toward her apartment. Loud, giddy laughter coming up from the lobby below made them turn to look as two figures ran across the floor and out through the front door.

"What the hell?" exclaimed Frances Wayne. "Jesus Christ, I swear that's them!"

"What? Who?" asked Matteo Amato.

"That nosey actress and her boyfriend, that's who. My, god!"

"Are you sure? I didn't get a chance to see them just now."

"Oh, yes, that was the two of them. What the *hell* were they doing here?"

"Stay here," said Amato, putting down the bag he was carrying. "Good timing. I'll take care of it. Loose ends. It might take a while, but I'll be back."

Matteo Amato raced down the stairwell and out into the parking lot. He watched as Billy Bennett closed Veronica's car door, as he had been gentleman enough to open it for her. Amato stopped running and walked casually to his car which was parked a few spaces away from Billy's. As far as he knew, neither Billy nor Veronica would recognize him. They certainly hadn't seen him at any time.

He got into his car and started the engine. Waiting.

The sky had grown dark, turning the late afternoon into an eerie early evening. A light rain began to fall and there was a flicker of lightning.

Amato saw the headlights turn on in Billy's car as it slowly started backing out of its parking space. He waited a few moments more.

Keeping an inconspicuous distance between them, Matteo Amato followed Billy's Oldsmobile as it headed out of town, driving through Parsippany toward Route 46 that would take them back to Dover.

Another car had pulled out of the parking lot, cautiously following Matteo Amato.

Traffic was light enough that it was easy to spot Billy's car even though the rain had turned, now, into a steady downpour. Amato assumed, correctly, that they would be heading back to Dover and he knew of a perfect spot on Route 46 where an "accident" might take place. He had caused a very similar fatal "accident" two years earlier and had gotten away with it. The unfortunate victim had been about to divulge some information to Lieutenant Gallagher regarding some unsavory business shenanigans in Dover involving Matteo Amato. He was a loose end.

The windshield wipers in Billy's car were going full force. He kept both hands firmly gripping the steering wheel when he glanced up into the rearview mirror.

"What the hell is that jerk doing?" he asked out loud.

Veronica turned around to look back.

The car behind them was coming extremely close. Too close.

The encroaching car suddenly flicked on its high beams, sending a blinding flash into both the rear view and side view mirrors and then into Billy's eyes. His pupils contracted. With the bright light coming through the raindrops streaming down the back window, the effect was dizzying. The lights flicked off and Billy's vision was in momentary darkness as his pupils dilated again. For a few seconds he saw spots before his eyes. The high beams flicked on once again and Veronica screamed.

"Billy, pull over or pull off the road, let that idiot pass us. What's he trying to do, kill us?"

Billy slowed down. There were very few other cars on the opposite side of the highway coming toward them, none with high beams on, but still Billy's eyes were affected. The car behind them pulled back.

"Whew, I guess he finally realized that he was being an asshole," Billy said, looking into his rearview mirror once again. "If he wanted to pass, why the hell didn't he just do so? Maybe he's drunk."

Although still driving with caution, he eased the car up in speed once again. The twisty road ahead was dark. There didn't appear to be any other car on either side of the highway. There were no houses or buildings of any kind on either side of the road, just trees. And darkness.

The car behind him flicked on his high beams once again, and then suddenly swerved out and came up along the driver's side of the Oldsmobile.

Taking a mere second for his vision to recover from that last blinding flash, Billy turned to look at the car to his left. It was keeping pace with his Oldsmobile 88 but it was slowly moving to the right, getting closer to it.

Billy tried to keep his eye on the dark road ahead, but he also kept glancing to the left as the car next to him inched closer.

Although he had hesitated at the dealership at the time, Billy was silently grateful now that he finally decided on getting the automatic instead of the manual transmission. At least he didn't have to contend with clutch, down shift, and brake. Clutch, shift, then gas as well as trying to avoid a disaster with a murderous driver.

Billy braked.

The car next to him braked. And then it inched even closer. And came closer still.

Peyton Chase was dining alone at Sallie's place. He had been reluctant right from the beginning to get involved with the mystery. He and Billy had had several discussions about it, with Billy Bennett agreeing wholeheartedly. But, alas, Billy was in love and Veronica had him tied up in knots. Had him by the balls, as Peyton Chase would say.

"Flyin' solo? Lover boy ditch ya tonight, flyboy?" Sallie asked as he came out from the kitchen. The rainy evening had kept the place quiet and only one other table was occupied.

"Yeah," answered Peyton, "Veronica is playing the Nancy Drew role tonight I'm afraid. Poor Billy got suckered in. I'm sure they'll be back home any minute. I hope. I thought they would be here by now."

"Want another beer?"

"Sure, why not, eh? It wasn't raining when I walked here, so I'll just sit it out for a while and see if it stops."

Sallie started walking back to the kitchen.

"No, wait," called out Peyton, "Forget the beer, how about a strong coffee and a cannoli?"

"You got it, pal," Sallie called over his shoulder.

There was a blinding flash of lightning outside, followed by a deep rumble of thunder. The rain was pelting the windows.

"I might be spending the night here!" Peyton called out to Sallie as he came out of the kitchen with the coffee and dessert. "I'll help with the dishes," he chuckled.

Another bright flash of lightning and an instant crack of thunder.

"Damn. That one was close," said Sallie, startled and almost spilling the coffee.

"Why the hell is he coming closer?" squealed Veronica. "What is he thinking?"

"He's thinking something very bad, Ronnie. *Very* bad. I have a horrible feeling that we might be very close to a murderer. Closer than we want to be at the moment!"

Billy didn't want his car to be scraped and he certainly didn't want to be involved in a nasty accident. The area was dark ahead. He cautiously pulled off the highway onto a shoulder. The gravel crunched under the tires as he slowed down but the car next to him kept coming closer. Billy didn't realize that there was a steep drop-off to the right of the shoulder. No guardrail to alert him to that matter. His car slid down the slicked grassy slope and tilted at an uncomfortable angle.

The offending car pulled off the road and onto the shoulder, avoiding the drop-off.

Matteo Amato turned off his lights and then the ignition. He didn't want it to look like his car might be in distress from any possible helpful passers-by, as few as they might be. He got out of his car after retrieving a revolver from his glove compartment.

In his side-view mirror Billy watched the silhouette of the man approaching the tilting car and his muscles tensed, the hair on the back of his neck rose. There was a flicker of lightning and Billy saw the gun. He recognized it immediately. It was a new six-round Colt Trooper, and he had just ordered a couple of them for their gun shop.

"Stay in the car and, for chrissake, get down, Ronnie. Please *don't* make a sound. That bastard has a gun."

Veronica's eyes widened and she scrunched down as far as she could go on the seat.

Matteo Amato approached the car slowly on the driver's side, gun raised.

There was no movement inside the car.

Billy waited, not moving a muscle, until the man was along side his door. Although it could possibly be a fatal mistake, with all the strength he could muster he suddenly thrust open the door slamming the man in his chest causing him to lose his balance and lose his grip on his gun. The gun went flying off down the slope as Billy leapt from the car.

Billy Bennett was ready for a fight. More than ready. Years of training.

Now without his weapon, Matteo Amato had to rely on his fists. Not his choice and not his strength. His first mistake was tensing his body, preventing him from maneuvering effectively.

Billy didn't take the time for a discussion or a reason, he just struck hard and quickly. Matteo Amato felt two swift blows in succession. First an upper cut to his chin hit him immediately, and then a swift left hook that had him momentarily dazed. Billy was driving each punch with his elbow rather than his fist and then exhaling sharply after each punch. This made him faster and more powerful.

Amato foolishly tried to kick Billy in the crotch but he was prepared for that and grabbed the man's leg, pushing him backwards and off-balance once again. He almost fell over but regained his stability quickly. Amato was afraid that he had bitten off more than he could chew with this guy but his anger swelled. He almost growled. He came right back at Billy, adrenaline pumping.

Amato landed a surprisingly powerful roundhouse right to the side of Billy's head making his left ear pound and ring like the bells of St. Mary's. He staggered back, shaking his head, but swiftly rebounded.

Billy remained focused. He immediately realized that his opponent was not really a good fighter just a lucky one. They danced around, trying not to slip or fall on the wet grass. It was still raining and lightning flickered overhead followed by low rolls of thunder. In his mind's eye, Billy Bennett was fighting a war once again. The opponent in front of him was a Nazi soldier, bent on beating him to a bloody pulp. The lightning was distant artillery fire and the thunder was the sound of bombs dropping. *Not gonna happen*, Billy thought.

They each swirled around, swinging, ducking, striking out at each other but not landing any blows. His anger reaching the boiling point, Billy lunged forward with his strong arms thrusting Matteo Amato up against the car with force. The door handle caught the man in his lower back inducing a painful yelp. Akin to a kidney punch. His knees nearly buckled. His nostrils flared and he stood erect again.

Veronica felt the sway of the car when the attacker had been pushed into it and she slowly sat up to see what was happening.

Billy quickly swung with his right once again but Amato ducked, avoiding the strike. Unfortunately he couldn't pull back in time and Billy's fist hit the car.

"Fuck!" he called out in pain.

Veronica thrust open her car door and leapt out into the pouring rain.

The sound of a distant siren caused them all to stop momentarily in their tracks. Billy holding his painful hand and Veronica rushing to his side.

The siren grew louder.

Matteo Amato suddenly abandoned the fight and ran up the slope to his car, turning to give one last glance at Billy and Veronica. The last thing he wanted was to be here when the cops showed up.

"I'm not finished with you two yet," he spat out in anger. "Your time is running out! Curtain's coming down, show's over, you actress bitch."

Lightning flashed as if to punctuate his statement. He gave them a rude finger gesture as he got into his car. He pulled slowly out into the passing traffic, trying to avoid being witnessed as fleeing from an accident.

"What was *that* all about?" cried a very upset and trembling Veronica Barron. "Who the hell was that, anyway?"

"I have no idea," responded Billy, rubbing his bloodied, painful knuckles. "But I feel fairly certain now that he knows *exactly* who *we* are. And I'm even more certain *how* and *why* he knows."

They stared at each other.

Thirty seconds later a Morris County police vehicle, with a flashing red light atop pulled up to the shoulder. The officer leapt from his vehicle and shone his search light down the slope. Billy and Veronica shielded their eyes as they stared back up at the officer as he made his way down toward them.

Someone had observed the incident from a short distance and alerted the police.

The rain had eased off so Peyton Chase decided to walk home from Sallie's. He was surprised that his roommates had not returned yet. He grabbed another beer from the refrigerator, took a big gulp, kicked off his shoes, and slumped down into an easy chair in the living room. He flicked on the radio beside him and was pleased to hear that his favorite show, *The Shadow*, was about to begin. But before he heard the maniacal laughter following those immortal words *"Who knows what evil lurks in the hearts of men? The Shadow knows!"* he had dozed off.

37

Peyton's eyes slowly fluttered open to the sound of the soulful musical theme from the movie *Laura* playing on the radio beside him. He glanced at his watch, then bolted upright. It was 3:25 A.M.

The lights were still on. The radio was still on. No one had poked him to wake him up and tell him to go to bed. Aside from the music, the apartment was quiet.

He got up from the chair and went down the hall to the bedrooms. The door to Veronica and Billy's dark bedroom was open.

"Guys?" he cautiously called.

No response.

He nervously reached in to flick on their bedroom light, only to discover that the bed was empty and, apparently, had not been slept in.

Not good, he thought to himself. *Not good at all.*

But he didn't know what to do.

Thinking there may be injuries, the police officer had radioed for an ambulance when he saw the car down the sharp incline. The medics, upon arrival, assessed the situation carefully. After introducing themselves, they quickly deduced that there were no apparent serious injuries to address. Billy Bennett and Veronica Barron were walking and talking, granted in a nervous, agitated state following the incident. If there had been an actual collision between any vehicles involved the injuries would certainly be far more obvious. They took the time to ask questions about the situation. The only blood that was evident was Billy's. They examined Billy's bruised and painful knuckles, especially the ones on his right hand, and confirmed that there were no broken bones. Badly and painfully bruised, to be sure. His left ear was slightly swollen, but the ringing had stopped.

"If, by any chance, you start to feel any discomfort or pain," said one of the medics, "don't hesitate to either see or call your respective doctors right away. There is always the possibility that you might feel it tomorrow in your neck, perhaps, or your back and legs, for example. I know there wasn't a collision, so no real trauma involved, but just in case…"

"No *trauma?*" screeched Veronica with just a hint of shaky sarcasm. "You call being run off the road by a murderous lunatic 'no trauma'?"

Billy looked at her.

"Ronnie," he simply said while shaking his head.

The two medics smiled and were as gracious as they could be.

"I understand, ma'am," one of them responded with a nod. "I didn't mean to sound callous in any way."

"We understand," Billy assured the medics. "And we certainly appreciate your swift attention here. "And I can also assure you that I won't be punching anyone else in the face for a long time."

"Let's hope not, sir," one of the medics laughed.

Determining no further injuries, they bade them goodnight, turned off their flashing lights, and drove off again into the night.

While awaiting the wrecker to arrive at the scene Officer Pendleton had tried to elicit as much information as possible from Billy Bennett and a still-shaken Veronica Barron.

Billy explained, as much as he could, about the incident. He had no idea who the other driver had been or why he was being driven off the road in that manner.

Actually, he *did* have a suspicion *why*, he just didn't know *who*. But he certainly wasn't willing to go into *that* long story.

"I only know, officer," said Billy, "that the man wanted to do some serious damage. And I mean *serious*. Not only did he run us off the road, and then he came at us with a gun. It was the Colt Trooper."

"And how do you know that?" asked the officer.

"An army buddy and I own a gun shop in Dover. We just ordered a few."

"No kiddin'?" responded Officer Pendleton matter-of-factly. "Most of us on the force have switched over to that piece. Nice little piece, too. Lighter and easier to handle than what we used before, for sure."

"Well, that bastard's little piece went flying down the slope over there before we went at it with our fists." Billy turned and pointed down into the darkness. "Want me to see if I can find it?"

"No, sir, you two just get into my car and relax. I'll see if I can find it for evidence."

"Relax? I'm not so sure I can relax in a police car," Veronica said nervously.

"Just get in the back seat to get outta the weather, ma'am. Keep the doors open if you'd rather. Be careful. If you close them, you won't be able to open them." And he laughed. He headed down the slope with a large flashlight.

"I didn't find that funny at all!" Veronica said as she stomped toward the police vehicle.

Veronica got in and slid over to the far side as Billy got in behind her.

"Okay, Ronnie, I know this is beating a dead horse but…"

"I know *exactly* where you think you're going with that one, cowboy, but don't."

Billy Bennett sighed, turning to look out into the darkness.

Veronica Barron put her elbows on her knees and buried her face in her hands, sobbing.

"Look at me," she cried. "I'm a mess and these are my brand new gabardine slacks!"

The wrecker that was called cautiously pulled Billy's car up from the slick, grassy slope. The rain slowly eased to a drizzle before finally ending. The storm had passed and the stars were beginning to appear overhead through the parting clouds. Much to Billy's relief, the car did not appear to be damaged in any way. He walked all the way around it inspecting it for scratches or scrapes. The sides were splattered with mud and bits of wet weedy grass, which would be remedied with a good hosing off combined with soap, water, and elbow grease. One of the hubcaps had popped off, but Billy found it further down the slope and retrieved it.

Peyton Chase paced the apartment. It was beginning to get light outside, with a bright sun breaking through the few remaining clouds. He knew that Billy and Veronica had headed to Morristown the evening before. He knew she was hoping to find the murdered woman's sister there. He knew that Billy had protested right from the start, before they had even left the apartment. What he *didn't* know was what had happened to them from that point on.

He didn't know who to call. He didn't know what to do. So he made a pot of coffee.

"I guess you could say that you two are lucky," said Officer Pendleton as he approached the car.

Billy and Veronica just stared at him.

"Yeah, this is a bad stretch of road along here. Lotta wrecks. There was another wreck, very similar to this one, along here about a year or so ago. Poor old guy didn't make it, though. His car rolled over a few times down this very slope. Looked like his car was sideswiped but the other car obviously sped off. Never located the bast..., sorry, ma'am...the other guy."

The officer was carrying the retrieved pistol by his pen that was protruding through the trigger guard. He reached into the front seat to get a paper evidence bag, carefully placing the revolver into it.

"Maybe we can get something from this," said Officer Pendleton holding the bag aloft. "Then again, maybe we can't. This might have been used in a recent crime elsewhere nearby. If we're lucky we might be able to pull some prints. Who knows, right?"

The wrecker had placed Billy's car directly in front of the police car.

After several more questions from the officer as he jotted down a lot of notes, Veronica started to open Billy's car door. She simply wanted to get in, get going again, and get home to a nice warm, dry, bed.

"Are we free to go, officer?" Billy asked. "We're through here, right? I can't think of any more that we could possibly tell you."

"Are you okay to drive, sir?" asked Officer Pendleton. "Do you feel safe about the car, I mean? Check all the components before pulling out onto the highway again. You know, like lights, brakes? Sure don't want you to start driving and have you car fall apart or anything, you know what I mean?"

Billy chuckled.

"I just want to get home. My girlfriend just wants to get home. My car looks fine at this point. I know there might be something about the car that I don't see, but I will be extremely careful, officer, trust me. I'll have it checked out by a mechanic as soon as I can."

"Okay, then," responded the officer. "Don't forget to notify your insurance company. I'll follow close behind for several miles just to play it safe. If you feel there's anything at all wrong with that car of yours, please, pull over and we'll make different plans, okay?"

"Absolutely, sir," Billy said, saluting the officer. "Thanks!"

There was light on the eastern horizon as Billy carefully drove off toward Dover.

38

It was almost time to go open the gun shop, but Peyton Chase was getting more concerned by the minute. His friends were still not home and he had no way to contact them, wherever they might be. Fearing the worst, he was pacing back and forth in the kitchen, finishing the last of his coffee, when he thought he heard the front door unlock and open. And then suddenly slam shut. He went running into the living room and stopped in his tracks. He could tell at a glance that there had been an altercation of some kind.

"Where the hell...? Peyton started.

"We *don't* want to talk about it," said Billy, red-faced and scowling. "Not now. Maybe *never!*"

Billy and Veronica, with her long blonde hair still dripping wet, stormed right past Peyton straight into their bedroom and slammed the door.

"And good morning to you, too," Peyton said with a dazed look on his face.

He simply shrugged his shoulders, grabbed his car keys and headed out the front door. Not slamming it.

He didn't notice it, but an unfamiliar car sat idling on the opposite side of the street two houses up the block. Waiting. Watching.

Peyton Chase ambled down their double driveway to get to his car. His beloved car. He had had this car, a 1941 Pontiac Streamliner Torpedo, before he went into the service and fought overseas. Veronica constantly referred to it as an old jalopy. Maybe it was, but he loved it nonetheless. He paid no attention to Billy's mud-splattered car parked next to his.

He slid in, shut the door and started the ignition. He had just put his foot on the clutch, shifting to reverse, when he noticed in the rear view mirror that a strange car had stopped out front blocking the driveway.

Matteo Amato had waited and cautiously, patiently followed Billy's car after the unsuccessful attempt earlier. Although he had lost his gun unexpectedly, he always kept a spare or two.

Peyton kept looking into the mirror as he slowly began to back up.

"Hey, asshole," he said out loud. "Move your fucking car."

The car didn't move. But the driver did.

In one swift motion, Amato popped from his car, raised his right arm and fired a revolver straight at Peyton's car, shattering the rear window.

Peyton Chase slumped over in his seat and, with his foot releasing the clutch, the car jerked and stalled to a sudden halt.

The sound of gunfire, shattering glass, and then squealing tires making a rapid getaway caused George Peer, their elderly landlord who lived upstairs, to throw open a window. He leaned out, looking down at the driveway.

"What in thunderin' tarnation is going on down there?" he yelled.

Bare-chested, barefoot, and wearing only his boxers, Billy raced out of the front door as he, too, had heard the commotion. He saw Peyton's car.

He slowly approached.

"Oh good god, no," he exclaimed as he walked closer.

Matteo Amato didn't know if he should simply drive around the block and wait to see if that pesky actress and her boyfriend come running out the house. He was certain he had killed their friend. Easy shot. The sun had reflected off of Peyton's rear window just before he fired his revolver, but Amato was positive he had hit his target anyway. They would surely rush to his car after they saw what had happened and he'd have a chance to get both of them before the police arrived. He was stopped by a traffic light when he heard a distant police siren. Thwarted again. He altered his plan and headed back to Morristown and Frances Wayne. He had been gone for hours.

Billy Bennett stopped in his tracks. Peyton Chase quickly sat up and pushed open his door with force.

"Goddammit!" he exclaimed with a grunt as he leaped from his car. "I'm reenlisting, for chrissake! It's safer in the frigging army than it is hanging around *you* two."

"Oh, jeez," said Billy with a sigh of relief. "When I heard that gunshot and saw your car..."

"Yeah, yeah," interrupted Peyton with a snarl. "I didn't know who that jerk was, but when I saw his hand bring out a gun I hit the deck fast. I reached up for the glove compartment to get my Berretta but before I knew it glass was raining down on me."

By this time Veronica, in her nightgown and robe, came running up to the two men.

"I just called the cops!" yelled George Peer from his upstairs window. "What in thunderin' tarnation!"

His wife, Betty, leaned over his shoulder and called down to the threesome. "Anybody hurt down there? Goodness, what a racket!"

"We're fine, Mrs. Peer. Aside from some rattled nerves," answered Billy.

"Yeah, and a smashed rear window," snorted Peyton. He leaned closer to look at his car. "Well, shit. Damn bullet went through my *front* windshield also."

"Maybe he was just trying to kill your old jalopy," said Veronica, trying to lighten the mood.

Peyton Chase glared at her. A withering look, at that.

"Not funny, Barron," he retorted. "Not funny at all. You sure as hell wouldn't be laughing if my dead ass was hanging out that car door."

Veronica rushed to his side and gave him a tight hug.

"I'm so sorry, Peyton, really I am. I guess my remark came out sounding too frivolous. I love you like a brother and I would be devastated...*truly* devastated if anything happened to you. Really."

They heard a siren in the distance as a patrol car approached.

"You know," said Billy, "I'm beginning to get really tired of hearing that sound."

A minute later a patrol car, red light flashing, pulled into the driveway behind Peyton's car. A police officer that was at least two sizes too large for his uniform slowly emerged from his vehicle and ambled toward the threesome in the driveway. He looked at Peyton's car and turned to look at Billy.

"I might suggest putting some clothes on there, son," he said, "before I have to write you up for public indecency."

Billy Bennett blushed. He had totally forgotten how he had raced from the house.

"Jeez, sorry officer, I'll be right back!" he said as he started a dash back into the house.

"I was only kidding, son, about fining you but some clothes might be nice," the officer said with a smile.

"Now then," he said turning to Peyton. "What's the situation here with your…"

He stopped speaking as another car pulled into the driveway behind his.

"What the…?" the office said with a bit of a surprise.

Detective Lieutenant Gallagher stepped out of the newly arrived vehicle. He made his way up the now-crowded driveway as Billy hurriedly rushed back out of the house buttoning up a shirt and making sure his fly was zipped.

George and Betty Peer, their interest now piqued, pulled up chairs by their upstairs window and leaned onto the windowsills, watching and listening intently.

"Lieutenant," asked the perplexed police officer, "what brings *you* here? I thought this was only some kind of domestic dispute or something."

"Well, it's *something*. But certainly a bit more than a domestic dispute, I'm afraid," answered Gallagher.

He turned to look, now, at Billy, Veronica, and Peyton.

"You seem to be a magnet for trouble," he said. "At least two of you are. Not sure I know how *you*," indicating Peyton, "figure into all this murder mess. But let's find out, shall we?"

The three friends just looked at one another, not knowing where this might be going now.

"Miss Barron and Mister Bennett," Lieutenant Gallagher began after clearing his throat, "I learned just a very short time ago that you two were involved in an incident last evening."

Peyton looked back and forth from Veronica to Billy. *He* did *not* know where this was going.

"Yes, sir," answered Billy sheepishly.

"And you, Mister Bennett, were injured. Correct?"

Billy held up his bruised fists, the right one especially looking rather red and ugly in the harsh morning light. Peyton looked at them as his eyes widened.

"Interesting scenario you two have gotten involved with, I must say," said Gallagher shaking his head. "Guess what we discovered?"

Billy and Veronica just stared, remaining silent.

"Some very quick detective work on our part was done overnight on that gun that was retrieved from the scene of your...umm...accident last night."

Silence, again, for a brief moment.

"And?" Veronica finally asked.

"It appears that it just happens to be the same gun that killed the former director of the Dover Preservation Society, Allyson Langston."

Because of the gunshot heard a short time earlier and the arrival of a police vehicle, several neighbors began coming out on the sidewalk to see what the situation was all about.

"Blue flies," said Gallagher, as he glanced in their direction. The other police officer laughed, nodding his head.

"Excuse me?" asked Billy.

"Blue flies swarm to piles of shit and to dead bodies. That's what we call all the onlookers who slow down to gawk at traffic accidents, hoping to see blood. An incident such as this one draws them, too. Blue flies. We have a lot more to discuss here. Can we perhaps go inside? Officer Shattuck," he said to the police officer beside him, "I'll move my car and you're free to go. I'll handle this situation for now."

George and Betty Peer stood up and slowly closed their window as they watched the patrol car back out of their driveway and head down the street.

"What in thunderin' tarnation?" said George Peer, shaking his head.

39

Even though he was still shaken and seething about his narrow escape and his damaged car, Peyton Chase immediately put on a pot of coffee to brew. He returned to the living room as Gallagher and his roommates were settling themselves. Billy Bennett and Veronica Barron sat side-by-side on the couch and Gallagher had seated himself in Peyton's favorite chair. Peyton silently grumbled, rolled his eyes, folded his arms across his chest, and sat on the arm of the couch.

"I love the aroma of coffee, don't you?" commented Lieutenant Gallagher with a smile as he flipped open his notebook. It was his way of trying to put everyone at ease.

Everyone else silently agreed but remained tense.

"Now then, you two," indicating Veronica and Billy, "what precipitated last night's events?"

Billy Bennett and Veronica Barron glanced at each other.

"That's *your* cue, Ronnie," said Billy, "hit it."

"Well...actually...I mean," she stammered. "Okay, I had a weird hunch that maybe Frances Wayne might be staying at her deceased sister's apartment in Morristown. From what little I was able to surmise from speaking with Alistair Stickle I thought perhaps she might be in danger, too, and was hoping to warn her about..."

"I'm going to stop you right there, Miss Barron," Gallagher interrupted. "Without going into too much detail here, and please pardon my abruptness, but unknowingly and foolishly you put yourself and your friend here," indicating Billy, "in serious jeopardy. You seem to be imprudently playing the role of detective without any sound reason. For your information, young lady, Brenda Barratt's sister, Frances Wayne, is not above suspicion here."

"What?" exclaimed an astonished Veronica.

"Who wants coffee?" asked Peyton. "This is beginning to get interesting!"

Lieutenant Gallagher raised his hand and nodded at Peyton. "Yes, sir. Black, please," he said.

Peyton brought the requested cup and sat back down on the arm of the couch, leaning forward, elbows on knees, to hear better.

Lieutenant Gallagher took a long sip of his coffee and set the cup down on the small table next to his chair.

"I, too, Miss Barron, have had a long conversation with Mr. Stickle, leading me to make more than just assumptions about Mrs. Wayne's involvement. The irony of the whole matter is that the chance meeting on an airplane between the deceased sister and your friend, Devon Stone, is slowly but surely bringing the whole situation into sharper focus. Your Mr. Stone, and his *unbelievable* memory, has helped in opening this case beyond that of a random killing in a posh New York hotel to one of a contentious and deadly family situation going back decades. His brief testimony to Lafferty of the NYPD set things in motion."

He stopped to take another sip of coffee.

"Describe for me, please, the guy that ran you off the road last night. The one you fought with," said the Lieutenant.

Peyton's head swirled around to look at Billy, his mouth agape. He, of course, knew nothing about this.

Billy described, as best he could, what the man looked like. Veronica filled him in with a few more details.

"Uh huh, sounds like that's the creep I suspected," said Gallagher, writing in his notebook. "And the one who tried to blast Stone to kingdom come last week. I know this jerk has a residence in London as well as one here in New Jersey. He's a slippery bastard. More than likely he followed you here after the incident last evening. I'm making a brash assumption that he's the one who shot up your car," indicating Peyton.

He finished off his coffee.

"Ah, good to the last drop. Thank you, sir," he said with a tip of his hand in a small salute to Peyton. "Oh, by the way young man. I do hope you can get that Pontiac of yours fixed up. She's a beaut. I have no doubt she'll be considered a classic in the years ahead. Mark my word."

Peyton arched his eyebrows, folded his arms across his chest and turned to Veronica, giving her that *See, I told you* kind of stare.

She stuck her tongue out at him.

"But we still don't know about the mystery," Veronica said, stopping the Lieutenant from leaving. "What *about* all those murders? What about that hideous painting? What about the forgery?"

"Miss Barron, I suggest that you get with Stickle about that. You will be in for an eye opening, I guarantee. For now, I have bigger fish to fry. His initials are M.A. Young lady; if you want my honest and blunt advice, stay the hell *out* of the detective business. Please. And, gentlemen, keep your powder dry."

"Jesus Christ!" screeched an irate Frances Wayne. "Four targets and you miss each one? Sure are getting sloppy, aren't you, Amato?"

Matteo Amato was just as distressed as Frances Wayne.

"Lousy circumstances, that's all," he moaned, lowering his head. "I know...time is running out."

"You're goddamn right about time. The contract expires tomorrow. I thought you'd have it all wrapped up by now. If any of them know anything and start to talk...you disappoint me. *Really* disappoint me."

"But..." he answered.

"Oh, stop," she barked. "No more. Get out! And maybe stay out."

"Our deal," Matteo Amato said with rising anger. "We've come this close. Don't you *dare* shut me out now, you bitch."

"And don't *you* dare threaten me," snapped Frances Wayne right back at him. "It won't end well if you do."

They glared at each other, words needn't be spoken but the message was clear.

"The painting?" Matteo Amato finally spoke.

"It's packed up securely and ready to be shipped to London. It's still here in the apartment. Don't worry about it. I have it handled," Frances Wayne said sharply, folding her arms across her chest.

"And the deal is..." Amato started.

"The deal is I'll decide when it's over. Now, as I said, get out!"

Matteo Amato balled his fists, noticed by Frances Wayne, but he relaxed. He slowly backed toward the apartment door.

"I'll be back," he snarled, slamming the door as he left.

Fueled by unmitigated hubris, Matteo Amato marched straight to his car in the apartment parking lot, seething all the way. He sat in his car and stewed for fifteen minutes, debating whether or not to go back in and finish the deal. Finish it in *his* way.

He played with the revolver in his hand for a few minutes before deciding not to do anything rash. Not today, anyway. He put the gun back into the glove compartment.

Let's see how this thing plays out, he thought to himself.

He started the engine and slowly pulled out of the parking lot.

A car that had been parked at the far end of the lot pulled out onto the road shortly after him and cautiously followed a safe distance behind.

40

June 2, 1953
The Contract Expires

Frances Wayne awoke with a raging headache. Today was a day long in coming and her deadly deal throughout the years with Matteo Amato would end. One way or the other. She no longer trusted him. But hadn't for several months recently. And since he couldn't follow through with dispatching the interlopers, how good was he in the long run?

But she realized how horribly ruthless the man was. What were *his* thoughts, especially following the harsh words spoken yesterday?

She didn't want to do anything she'd regret but she felt as though she might need to protect herself. She had seen Amato's rage in the past.

Although she hadn't used it in ages, she kept a loaded pistol in her purse. Just in case.

Matteo Amato had let his anger fester and grow throughout the night. He had trusted Frances Wayne and was eager for the deal to reach its conclusion. But would she end it the way they had planned? He had lost faith in her over the past few weeks. He had thought that the murder of Brenda Barratt would be the icing on the cake and things would proceed perfectly from there on. No witnesses. Nothing to trace the crime to him. If only. A conversation on an airplane. A mystery writer. A meddling bimbo and her boyfriend. And now, Frances Wayne seemed to be turning on him at the last minute. With millions at stake!

Instead of returning to his own apartment following his argument with Frances Wayne, he felt that just perhaps a particular police lieutenant might know where he lives and come calling. Renting a room in a cheap motel on Route 46 not too far from Morristown, he had had a restless night. But he was ready to face the day, come what may. Today was a coin flip: good luck, bad luck. He showered and dressed. He stared at himself in the bathroom mirror. The thoughts flowed. If something just might happen to Frances Wayne today…say, a fall down a flight of stairs in the dark stairwell at the apartment building…or, perhaps a bereaved sister committing suicide by tumbling over the railings from the third floor.

They wouldn't need to split the proceeds then. He smiled at himself. And his ego-inflated reflection smiled back.

"Why don't you stay home today," Peyton Chase said to Billy. "Look at your knuckles. They still look nasty. Jesus, you must have clobbered him good the other night."

"I clobbered my *car* good, that's for damn sure," answered Billy Bennett. "No, why don't *you* stay home? You're the one who got shot at yesterday."

They both thought about it for a minute.

"I'll call my dad," said Peyton. "We never did open up yesterday after all that commotion. He can open the shop today. Make him happy. He loves it when I call on him for that. Then we can both stay home. And drink."

"Good idea, buddy. *Great* idea!"

Frances Wayne knew as soon as she opened the door to her apartment that Matteo Amato was up to no good. Her regrets instantly raced through her mind. Regretted letting him into her life. Regretting letting him in on her plan. Regretted letting him into the apartment just now.

Matteo Amato stepped into the apartment and started walking toward her, leaving the door open behind him.

Frances Wayne was prepared. Her purse was on an end table next to her and she quickly reached in pulling out her pistol.

"Oh Jesus," snickered Amato. "A familiar scenario for me. And helps with a little problem I thought I had. Dimwit Alice Rose pulled the same trick with me not too long ago. And you see how *that* ended."

Frances Wayne *did* know how that had ended. The newspapers had said suicide. But she knew better.

He started walking toward her...taunting her. He was ready to reach out, grab her arm and force the barrel of the pistol in the woman's mouth. Contract expired. End of deal. All his!

"Don't come any closer," she said, almost trembling.

As he made a step toward her, she raised the pistol. That action made no difference. He smiled and took another step. He couldn't ever imagine that she would actually shoot him.

He was mistaken.

He reached out toward her and she fired. She watched in horror as the red blotch grew on his chest, oozing through his thin shirt. He staggered, shocked, backward out the open door. The railing to the balcony behind him didn't stop his movement. He couldn't stop the momentum and he disappeared over it, falling the three flights to the floor of the lobby below where his skull cracked open, splattering blood and brain matter.

She ran to the railing, looked down, and saw him lying there, contorted, motionless on the white marble floor surrounded by a widening pool of blood. Not believing that she had really and truly shot him, still brandishing her gun she blindly raced down the spiraling steps of the four-sided stairwell stopping only when she breathlessly reached the last step. She burst though the door into the lobby and stood there in shock and confusion.

A gun was pointed squarely at her chest and standing before her was a younger version of the man she had just killed.

"Thanks," said Matt Amato as he lowered his gun. "You just saved me the trouble and years of therapy and incarceration."

"What?...wait...but...who the hell are *you?*" asked a bewildered Frances Wayne.

"I'm assuming you *are* responsible for my father's death just now, right?" said the young man.

Frances Wayne stared in total shock at the young man. Then looked down at the dead man on the floor. She started backing away, shaking her head.

"Matteo had a *son?*" was all she could say, almost as a whisper. "What the *hell?*"

"You never knew?" asked Matt Amato arching his eyebrows in surprise. "Huh, after all these years you never knew. Of course not. He never told you, did he?"

It looked as though Frances Wayne was about to crumble.

"He was such a bastard," said Matt. "I loathed and feared him for years. And he hated and ignored *me* for years. Until recently. When he needed me. Or needed my talent, that is. Where do you think he got that reproduction of *Memento Mori*, the Five and Ten? I have been following him for some time now and I knew what you two were doing regarding the paintings, but I never figured that murder would be a part of it. I was mistaken and for that I am truly ashamed. The authorities should have been alerted much sooner."

All of a sudden Frances Wayne regained her vile composure. She quickly realized that this young man changed the dynamic. Her vindictive mind was racing. She raised her gun once again.

"I killed your goddamned father in self-defense," sneered Frances Wayne. "He came after me, and it will appear that you did, too. I can say that both you and your stupid father tried to kill me. You're holding a gun now. I can kill *you* in self-defense."

"No, you can't," came a voice several feet behind her.

41

Startled, Frances Wayne spun around to confront the voice. She froze.

"Hello, Aunt Frances," said Alistair Stickle.

Her plan was unraveling right before her eyes. *How could this be happening*, she thought. *Not now. Christ almighty, not now!*

The years of planning. The years of waiting. Gone. Her quiet, simple but malevolent plan had turned to chaos in a flash.

"Son of a bitch, for years I thought you were dead," a now nearly hysterical Frances Wayne hissed. "We *all* thought you were dead. Hoping and praying that you *were* dead. Why didn't you *stay* dead…or stay wherever the hell you were…?"

She raised her gun, now pointed straight at Alistair Stickle.

"No!" cried out Matt Amato frantically, rushing forward pushing Frances Wayne and knocking her off balance ruining her aim. The sudden jolt caused her to pull the trigger.

Alistair Stickle, stumbling backwards, grabbed his leg above his knee and watched the blood flow down his pants leg. He painfully crumpled to the floor Fortunately the bullet had missed his femoral artery.

Not waiting for even a second, an enraged Frances Wayne spun around once again and had her gun poised to blast Matt Amato in his head. Her eyes instantly widened in stunned surprise as her body jerked. She felt the sudden hot pain at practically the same time she heard the gunshot. And then there was silence. The pain was in the center of her upper back but the blood was coming out the front of her chest, reddening her blouse as she looked down at it. Her legs went limp. Losing the feeling in her fingers, she dropped the gun. Her body crumpling, she melted down onto the floor like the Wicked Witch that she was.

As she fell she weakly moaned the very last words that she would ever say. "Memento… Mori."

Remember… you must die.

Lieutenant Gallagher lowered his just-fired revolver. Alerted by someone a couple hours earlier that something big was about to happen here, he had come into the building and entered the atrium at just the right moment.

The atrium in the building was soon abuzz with gasps, a couple scattered screams, and loud chatter from the confused, frightened apartment dwellers as they rushed from their doors. The sound of the gunfire had reverberated through the expansive interior. Many of the people leaned over the railings on the various floors to see what might be happening below. A few women turned away from the railings in horror as they saw three bodies on the floor of the atrium. An elderly woman on the fourth floor landing, who appeared ready to faint, was led back into their apartment by her husband. Blood was flowing in spreading pools from two apparently dead bodies and one man appeared to be writhing in pain on the floor.

Matt Amato had rushed to Alistair Stickle's side, kneeling down; trying any way he could to apply pressure to stop the flow of blood.

"Ambulance is on the way, son," Gallagher said looking down at the two men. "Hang on."

Lieutenant Gallagher looked up into the atrium and scanned the faces of dozens of residents. Blue flies.

"They'll be talking about this for years to come," he said practically to himself, shaking his head. "What a fucking mess."

He returned his gaze to the two men on the floor. As if he had just seen Matt Amato for the first time he cocked his head. He looked confused.

"Well now. And who the hell are *you*?" he asked.

"Seems like I've heard that before, sir. I've remained in the shadows, but you and I have spoken on the telephone recently, Lieutenant."

Lieutenant Gallagher smiled…and nodded.

42

Had the murderous Frances Wayne remained alive, she would have been very disturbed, and furious, to hear what actually *was* in Brenda Barratt's will. She had made what she thought was an obvious assumption at the time. She was the sole survivor of the family after all these years and would, therefore, inherit everything despite the fact that their relationship had become a fractious one. But Frances Wayne never had the chance to meet with her lawyers or Brenda Barratt's lawyers before her dramatic departure from life.

Prior to her recent trip to London, Brenda Barratt had a new will drawn up. She had strong suspicions that her contemptuous sister had been behind the manipulations of the values regarding the works of the old artist, Matteo Amato. Should she, Brenda Barratt, be the oldest surviving member of Grover Sutton's family on the day the contract expired, she would retrieve the hideous painting from the Dover Preservation Society. As much as she wanted to have the painting destroyed, no matter the current value, she had a very strong sense that her beloved grandson, Alistair Stickle, was still alive somewhere.

Upon her death then, all of Brenda Barratt's possessions which included, among substantial financial holdings, fine jewelry, several pieces of exquisite contemporary artwork, as well as dozens of rare and highly valued antique paperweights, would be sold...with the exception of the painting *Memento Mori*. The entire proceeds, which would amount to slightly over two million dollars, were to be bequeathed to the Museum of Modern Art in New York City in the name of her father, Grover Sutton. A legacy of love and beauty replacing the fifty-year legacy depicting somber death.

Memento Mori would be held aside and given to Alistair Stickle, should he still be alive, to do as he so desired.

43

"This might sound more complicated than it really is," Matt Amato said as he sat next to Alistair Stickle's hospital bed. "Then again, the whole deal frazzled *my* mind when I first heard about it. And, unfortunately, I was brought in as a kind of a distraction. Trust me, Al; I had no idea that murder would be a part of the charade. I would have called the cops without hesitation and put the kibosh on it in a flash."

"Do we need to draw a flow chart?" asked Alistair Stickle, almost as a joke.

They both chuckled but then quickly regained the gravity of the situation.

"Okay then, let's get serious here," Alistair began. "After my parents were killed, I realized that something very sinister was happening. Maybe I was being stupid…I don't know. What I did was illegal, certainly. Got a fake passport, changed my identity and hightailed it to Europe."

"I take it that you may have realized, then, that it must have had something to do with the situation regarding that painting at the Preservation Society, didn't you?" asked Matt. "Well, very astute of you, I must say. You must have known at that time that eventually the painting would end up with the sole survivor in your family."

"True," answered Alistair, "Up to a point. I tracked the sales of your grandfather's paintings from country to country over the past seven years. It wasn't easy, believe me. They might have been in either some local auction houses or little art galleries."

"Seriously? Are you telling me that some of them ended up in Mauritius and Tahiti?" asked an incredulous Matt Amato.

"Well, actually, no. I just got tired of tracking them and wanted a nice safe, peaceful place to remain for a while. So I continued travelling eastward. I stopped over in Mauritius for a while but didn't like it. Not private enough, so I continued on to the sister island of Tahiti. I started painting again and even fell in love. It also gave me time to think about what might be going on regarding all those paintings done by your grandfather. What struck me as odd were the unnaturally exorbitant prices they generated. That certainly threw up a red flag for me."

"As well it should," responded Matt Amato. "Obviously you figured out that someone must have been manipulating the prices of the artwork. Bidding outrageous prices to increase the value of my grandfather's other works."

"Exactly," said Alistair Stickle, "but I could never get a read on who that person or persons were. The bidding was done anonymously. I had my suspicions, though."

"You thought it was me, didn't you?" asked Matt. "I mean, not only for that, but for the murder of your parents."

There was a pause and Alistair looked down. Embarrassed.

"Yes. I did," Alistair finally answered. "And I voiced those suspicions to our other Ghost Army buddy, Tony Dunlap, and to that actress who has been out there playing detective."

"My father and I were at odds for years," sighed Matt Amato. "Aside from the fact that he ridiculed my desire to become a fine artist, he despised me because…well, maybe you already suspected this. Then again, maybe not." Matt paused and took a deep breath. "God, this is not an easy confession. He despised me because I had boyfriends instead of girlfriends. I didn't flaunt it. I tried to be as discrete as possible."

Alistair Stickle smiled and put his hand on Matt's shoulder.

"Yeah, I may have had my suspicions, Matt, from time to time. Certain, I don't know… certain little behaviorisms," he said, maintaining eye contact with his friend, "but you know what? I didn't care. It didn't bother me one little iota. Live and let live, as someone far more important than you or me once said."

Matt Amato, eyes glistening, smiled broadly at his friend.

There was one thing that, now, Matt Amato knew he would never share with Alistair Stickle. During the war when they first met in France, when he had first seen this shirtless, handsome young man helping with an inflatable tank, there had been an attraction that Matt Amato knew would never…*could* never be returned. The attraction was still there. Renewed once he saw his friend again. But the handsome, well-tanned man now lying there in the hospital bed in pajamas would never know.

"We, meaning you and me, Al, fought side-by-side during World War II. The Nazis reviled men like me as much as they hated the Jews. Homosexuals were rounded up, put into concentration camps and branded with a pink triangle on their clothing. I've always been scared to death about being exposed. Remember, my kind of love is illegal. My father capitalized on that in the most heinous of ways."

"A sort of blackmail? His own son?"

"He was a despicable man, Al. Through and through. He taunted me. Said that if my beloved mother hadn't already been dead, finding out that I was a queer would have killed her. He was never bold enough...or dumb enough to be in the Mafia although for the longest time I thought he was. I never, ever realized that he was capable of murder...several of them, at that."

"Yet, you did what he asked, didn't you? You forged *Memento Mori* for him."

"Yes, I did."

"Why?"

"Because I knew then that I was going to kill him. And I would have. I was prepared to do it. Fortunately Frances Wayne beat me to it."

44

Veronica and Devon encountered a sullen Matt Amato as he was leaving his friend's hospital room. They chatted briefly and he agreed to wait for them down in the lobby.

"There's no need for that," said Alistair Stickle after Veronica told him about needing to get more information from the library about something called the Avenue of Death.

He tried to prop himself up as much as he could in the uncomfortable hospital bed. It was obvious that his wounded leg pained him with every move.

"I knew only part of the story regarding my great-grandfather and that wretched painting. Evidently my poor grandmother shielded me from the truth. She tried to spare me the horrific details. Matt filled me in with all the missing puzzle pieces. Sorry you missed him."

"We just saw him a few seconds ago in the hallway outside your room," said Veronica. "We'll catch up with him later."

Alistair Stickle tried to get comfortable once again but it didn't appear to be working. Veronica and Devon moved closer to the bed. They knew a story was about to be told.

"Oh, I'm so sorry that your boyfriend got banged up a bit," Alistair said, wincing as he tried to move over. "And your other friend's car got damaged."

"Don't worry about them," Veronica said, waving it off. "They'll be fine. At least neither one of them was shot this time."

"*This* time?" asked Alistair.

"Long story," Veronica answered. "We'll save it for another day. And you were saying about those puzzle pieces?"

A very officious-looking nurse quickly entered the room. She stood at the end of the bed, tapping her foot and folded her arms.

"Visiting hours are just about over, folks, and I have to change the dressing on his wound, so…"

"So buzz off for ten minutes, will ya?" said Alistair Stickle sternly. "These friends need to hear something that you do *not*. So back out of the room and come back when they leave. I promise that I'll be a good boy and not scream *too* much when you apply that awful salve."

The nurse huffed, and then spun on her heels muttering something under her breath as she left.

"And she's one of the friendlier ones here," Alistair chuckled.

He reached for a glass of water, discarding the bent straw, and took a long gulp.

"Is this going to be a sad story?" asked Veronica.

"Oh, yes, my dear friend. Feel free to weep. You can weep too, Devon, if need be."

"I'm made of sterner stuff, lad," answered Devon Stone. "Remember, I kill for a living. On the printed page, that is."

Devon Stone and Veronica Barron exchanged glances and a quick wink.

"You two were quite correct to deduce that this whole ordeal started way back in 1903, just before Grover Sutton, my great-grandfather, loaned that painting. A painting that no one can understand why anyone in his or her right mind would want."

Alistair Stickle took another sip of water and Veronica could see that tears were beginning to well in his eyes.

"It was because of guilt and shame," he sighed deeply. The Avenue of Death was a real place. Well, it was a small section of Manhattan that was nicknamed that from the late 1800s into the early 1900s. Two streets, actually, running parallel. Tenth and Eleventh Avenues on Manhattan's west side. Horribly congested and dangerous, not only with automobiles, trucks, horse carts, and pedestrians but, to make it even more hazardous, actual steam trains. Yes, believe it or not railroad tracks ran right down the center of these two streets. The trucks and trains carried various items such as produce, dairy products, beef, and even coal to the warehouses along the way. Because of all the congestion, accidents and multiple deaths over the years ensued, hence that dreadful epithet."

Veronica wondered where this might be going. Devon began to formulate a possible scenario in his mind.

"My great-grandfather was extremely wealthy. That much I have known for years. How he made his money is anybody's guess at this point. I was never made privy to that fact. It may have been "old money" for all I know. Doesn't matter. Bear in mind, one million dollars in 1903 would be equivalent of at least three times that now. But his fortune was *much* more than one million. He also had the sad *mis*fortune of driving along Eleventh Avenue at the wrong time. In the wrong place. Matteo Amato, the elder...the now-infamous painter, had a young daughter with a toddler son. The little boy was four-years old. They, too, were in the wrong place, with unfortunate timing. The youngster broke away from his mother's arms running to pet a horse he saw on the opposite side of the street. My great-grandfather saw him too late to apply his brakes, running into him and crushing the young boy's skull. The child died in his mother's arms as, I was told, she wailed like a banshee. Dozens of witnesses attested to my great-grandfather's innocence, of course. It had been a horrendous accident."

He stopped to take a breath.

"But it didn't stop there. The grief-stricken young mother committed suicide the following week."

Veronica had a hand up to her mouth.

Devon lowered his head.

"My great-grandfather was a decent, God-fearing man. He was devastated by the ordeal. Money certainly cannot replace a young life, but he and his lawyers met with Matteo Amato and fashioned a financial agreement that would run for fifty years. A trust fund would pay $500.00 per month to Matteo Amato or his surviving direct descendants until 1953. Of course, $500.00 *then* was a hell of a lot of money. You could buy a brand new car for just a little bit more than that."

"But..." started Veronica.

Alistair held up his hand.

"Wait," he said, "I wasn't finished. That is, Matteo Amato wasn't finished. His taste in subject matter had already been pretty grim and grotesque. Needless to say, he, too, was beyond inconsolable. While he appreciated and readily accepted the gesture of the money, he did not consider that it was enough reparation for the suffering his family had endured. He made an offer…no, actually it was a demand. He would paint a special painting that my great-grandfather would purchase at a fair price and instantly place on display and loan to the Dover Preservation Society to run concurrently with the trust fund monies. Agreement was made. The contract was signed and would expire on June 2, 1953. The fiftieth anniversary of Amato's daughter's suicide. And, as you know, that painting is *Memento Mori*. Matteo Amato wanted my great-grandfather's name, Grover Sutton, to be forever linked to that image. Death."

The room fell silent.

45

"Okay, so that explains about the painting," Veronica started. "But why all these murders?"

"That's where the fun part comes in," answered Alistair Stickle.

"*Fun* part!" Veronica gasped with mouth agape.

"I do believe, my dear Veronica," chimed in Devon Stone, "that a heavy dose of sarcasm was just injected there."

"Right," smiled Alistair. "Obviously too many people were learning too many things about the original deal. And any one of those folks could have spilled the beans at any time. Matteo Amato, the old painter, and Grover Sutton were both extremely shrewd businessmen. They, along with the lawyers representing the Dover Preservation Society at that time, created a well-thought out arrangement trying to circumvent any potential miscreants throughout the decades."

"Are we all to understand that the details of said arrangement were kept secret for the past fifty years?" asked Devon Stone with a frown.

"Secret from the public, of course," answered Alistair Stickle. "I knew only a smattering. My poor grandmother had told me certain things. My fellow-ghost, Matt, filled me in on most of the rest. But what my grandmother told me seemed innocuous at the time. Until the murders began…starting with those of my parents. Time was running short on the contract. And the deal was that the painting *must* remain hanging at the Society throughout the years until June 2, 1953 or the money instantly stops going to the remaining surviving Amato family. Upon the termination date of the deal, should there be no surviving members of *my* family…Grover Sutton's family…the painting was to be destroyed."

"Poor choice of words there, lad," said Devon. "Termination date. Appropriate, surely, but still sounds sinister considering all that has happened recently."

Veronica sat silent for a moment, trying to let all this information sink in.

"But…" she finally said.

"*But*," interrupted Alistair Stickle, "that's why Matt Amato's murderous father had him paint a forgery. And a damn good one at that. It was an insurance policy of sorts. Just in case the painting was actually destroyed. It would have been the forgery that was destroyed and not the original that was now worth one million dollars."

"Could this story get any more convoluted?" Devon said, shaking his head.

"Two more tidbits and we'll bring this to a close," smiled Alistair. "A twisted tale, for damn sure!"

"I'm not sure I comprehend all this yet," said a bewildered Veronica Barron.

"Wait for the movie, my dear," chuckled Devon, "maybe that will make everything more understandable."

"Are you ready for the big revelation?" asked Alistair. "The term *twisted* doesn't cover it. My beloved grandmother's sister, my wretched, murderous great-aunt Frances, and Matt's father were lovers. Had been for years. I don't know if her late husband was aware of her indiscretions or not. Doesn't matter. Who knows? Maybe she discretely murdered him, too. I have no idea when or how he died. She was evil through and through. She and Matteo Amato had grown richer together throughout the years because of that monthly trust fund deal and very shrewd investments. Evidently she had concocted this whole scheme and she, anonymously, bid on all and bought some of the elder Amato's paintings…bidding them up outrageously, so she and her lover would eventually end up with a painting worth one million dollars. Obviously, then, her entire collection of his paintings would have kept them rolling in dough for years to come. I can only speculate at this time that my grandmother was either suspicious or was aware of what Aunt Frances was doing to manipulate the prices. Perhaps that's why you all became targets. Maybe Aunt Frances and Amato feared that Brenda Barratt told you, Devon, some of that devious plan on the plane and you could alert the authorities or the media at any time. If you had in that case, probably the value of all those Amato paintings would deflate faster than a pricked balloon."

He paused to take a breath and ponder one other thought.

"Knowing my grandmother, I feel certain she wanted to retain ownership of that painting so she could destroy it, no matter the value. She would have wanted to erase my great-grandfather's name from that tragic legacy. But, again, I'm only speculating. The truly weird part… well, even *more* weird than all the rest… Matteo never told Frances that he even *had* a son. She knew that he was a widower. His wife had died from a massive heart attack years earlier. All of his other relatives were, supposedly, dead. He was the sole survivor. She knew that he could be treacherous. But then, so could she. Consequently and sadly they ended up not trusting each other."

"And, consequently," added Devon, "they ended up dying within minutes of each other."

"Coincidence or not, their lives ended on the very day the contract expired," said Alistair Stickle shrugging his shoulders. "Should you ever decide to write a book with this scenario, Devon, you might want to add one more odd tidbit of trivia. That fifty-year contract expired yesterday, on June 2, 1953. And, as I'm sure you are well aware, that was the day of *your* new Queen's formal inauguration in London. A worldwide celebration of a new beginning. Ready for this? And, as we also now know, Amato's daughter committed suicide on June the 2, 1903. Her name happened to be Elizabeth.

Five minutes later Lieutenant Gallagher entered the hospital room, followed by an irate nurse.

"I told everybody thirty minutes ago that visiting hours are *over!*" huffed the nurse waving her arms around. "Now go! All of you."

Gallagher flashed his badge at her and she suddenly closed her mouth. But she folded her arms across her chest and tapped one foot angrily.

"Good evening, again, everybody," said the smiling Lieutenant. "How are *you* doing, young man?" he asked of Alistair Stickle as he walked up to the side of the bed.

"Not ready to dance a jig anytime soon, Lieutenant, but all things considered I'm doing just great."

Lieutenant Gallagher cleared his throat and inhaled deeply.

"I know you've been through a nasty ordeal. Years of it, I guess. My sympathies are with you. And I understand completely. No doubt the details of which would frazzle my mind." He paused briefly. "That being said…"

And everyone seemed to know what was coming next.

"Seven years ago you fled from the scene of a nasty crime. Granted, you were innocent but nevertheless, that was unacceptable. And *then* you fled the country utilizing a fake passport. That, too, was unacceptable. Illegal. Serious crime, there, guy. Serious. I had to do my duty and notify the appropriate authorities. I explained the entire situation to them. I doubt, however, that they will be as understanding about things as I have been."

The mood in the room had become somber. Veronica Barron was now on the verge of tears. Devon Stone knew about the consequences. The nurse unfolded her arms.

"Sometime tomorrow, don't know what time, but you will be visited by some stern government folks," continued Gallagher. "I wish I could say that it will be a pleasant visit. I'm sorry, son, but I had to do my duty as an officer of the law."

"I completely understand, Lieutenant," said Alistair nodding his head and shrugging his shoulders. "I was in the wrong. I was foolish. I'm surprised that the hammer hasn't come down on my head before this. And I will certainly *not* hold it against you. After all, sir, you saved my life and that of my buddy, Matt. I will be eternally grateful."

46

Billy Bennett and Peyton Chase were waiting in the hospital lobby for Veronica and Devon to join them. Veronica gave them the short version of the story she and Devon had just heard upstairs. In one respect, the little group of friends was relieved that the mystery was solved and the murders had come to an end. But on the other hand, they were concerned for what lay ahead for Alistair Stickle. They had left his hospital room knowing that the authorities wouldn't be an understanding lot, even considering the circumstances.

Matt Amato saw the group and joined them.

"I need to get home and relax," said Veronica. "My head is about to explode."

"I need a drink," said Billy. "That story is too much to take. I've had it with all this murder shit!"

"I need a drink just because my buddy here," indicating Billy, "needs one!" said Peyton.

"I need to get home, and I mean to London!" sighed Devon Stone. "I've had more than enough of this nonsense and I have a book to finish. I may even hesitate to set foot back on this continent for my upcoming book tour."

"I'm spending the night with a good friend down in Greenwich Village," said Matt Amato, "so I'll be very glad to drive you in to your hotel or out to Idlewild if you have a flight already, Devon."

"I shall gladly accept the offer of a ride into the city, young man," answered the author. "But, being that you're headed to the Village, do you know of a tavern called McSorley's by any chance?"

"As a matter of fact I do. Not too far from my friend's place, actually. I think you'll find it fascinating. Old, dingy, filled with decades of history, for sure. Abraham Lincoln even had a drink or two there, I hear."

"I'm intrigued. A little research never hurts. Who knows? I shall take my chances and if I'm lucky I might even run into that dapper Lieutenant Lafferty. He told me it's one of his favorite hangouts. I'm sure he must know about all the murderous details by now. But I'd like to see him one last time. I need to probe him a little more for future writings. He'll make an interesting character."

"Well," chuckled Matt Amato, "don't expect to flirt with any pretty barmaids there. Women are strictly prohibited from entering the premises."

Devon's eyes widened.

"Not that I would flirt with them anyway," Matt Amato laughed.

"Well, then, just drop me off at the bar if you wouldn't mind. And I want to have a brief chat with my publisher in the morning and then I'll see about a flight eastward. Let me say my goodbyes to my pesky friends and we shall be on our way, right?"

After hugs, handshakes and a big kiss from Veronica Barron, Devon Stone opened the door to Matt's car.

Billy Bennett and Peyton Chase stood back, side-by-side, in the parking lot and watched as Veronica ran up to Devon for one last kiss.

"Hey, Devon," Billy called out laughing, "if we happen to hear of any more good murder plots for you…"

"…We'll duct-tape Veronica's mouth shut!" finished Peyton with a louder laugh.

Veronica honored that remark with a rude gesture involving her middle finger.

"Grow up, you two," she snorted, heading toward Billy's car.

Traffic was light and Matt Amato appeared downtrodden as they drove into the city. Because of the limited but somber chat as they drove, Devon Stone could see that the young man was still tormented about his family's murderous ways and felt responsible or at least contributed to the horrendous outcome in some way.

"You have nothing to regret, my young friend," said Devon, reaching over and putting his hand on Matt's shoulder, squeezing it gently. "You were oblivious, I'm sure, to where the deeds would lead. But look *forward*, not back. You no longer have to fear the shadow of your father. Just embrace the fond memory of your grandfather's love. You have an incredible talent for painting. Now use it for the good. You've been given a second chance, lad; it's called tomorrow. As another friend, wise philosopher and fellow writer, Allan Watts, recently said: *You are under no obligation to be the same person you were five minutes ago.* The Grover Sutton and elder Matteo Amato epoch is over. Move on, young man, move on."

"Easier said than done, Devon, as *that* old expression goes," answered Matt Amato.

"Ain't *that* the truth, as you Yanks might say," answered Devon Stone. "I know what I just told you probably sounds trite. Well, it *is*. And perhaps you're thinking it's just a bit too sanctimonious. And perhaps you're correct about *that* as well. But it's still worthwhile."

They both smiled.

"Now that Stickle has graciously given that damnable painting to you, what are your intentions? Any ideas yet?" asked Devon.

A moment of thoughtful silence.

"The way I see it, Devon, I have only three options. Sell it. Donate it. Destroy it. I sure as hell don't want to keep it. But once the press gets word of the true facts regarding this outrageous situation, I have a feeling that the over-inflated value of that quote-unquote masterpiece will soon vanish in a puff of smoke."

Devon Stone thought that there was one other possibility that young Matt Amato had not even considered. Human nature and curiosity being what it is, the value of the grotesque painting *could* have doubled.

The car pulled up to the front of McSorley's Old Ale House on East 7th Street and stopped. Devon Stone looked out of the car window at the place. *Established 1854* read the sign beneath the tavern's name. It *did* look old and dingy but, from what could be seen through its old dirty windows, it was doing a brisk and rowdy business. Laughter spilled out through the front door. A door that looked ready to fall off its hinges.

The two men got out and faced one another on the sidewalk.

"No matter what I decide, Devon, I *am* grateful for your thoughtful advice. Please don't take offense at this, but I have never read any of your books. For that matter, before the shenanigans of the past few weeks I never even knew who you were. And *because* of the shenanigans of the past few weeks I will never, *ever* read any of your books. I want *nothing* to do with murders in any way or form. No books. No movies. And for the rest of my life I won't even kill time."

Devon Stone couldn't help laughing.

"Thanks, lad, that's a hoot. No offense taken. Have fun down here in the Village with your friend tonight. Have a good life. Be sensible. Be careful. Be proud."

The two men shook hands and then Devon Stone stood in silence as he watched the young man get back into his car and pull away from the curb, driving off into his future. He turned, sighed, and then walked into the tavern wondering what challenges might lay ahead for young Matt Amato now that the challenges of his past were soon to be buried. But something in his gut told Devon Stone that he need not worry about Alistair Stickle.

Because by daybreak the next morning Alistair Stickle will be nowhere to be found. The ghost will have vanished once again.

47

Billy Bennett was soaking in a bathtub filled with steaming hot water but he had laid a pan filled with ice cubes, cold water and Epsom salt on the rim of the tub. His right hand was submerged in the pan. He hated the cold but it was the best way to help ease his still-bruised and sore knuckles. He switched positions in the tub every few minutes so he could place his left, and equally bruised hand into the pan. He reacted with a startled jump and a splash when the bathroom door was suddenly thrust open and Veronica Barron came running in, her arms aflutter.

"You will not believe this," she practically yelled with excitement. "You simply will *not* believe it!"

"Oh, try me," said Billy with annoyed sarcasm. "Unless you've uncovered yet another damn murder."

"Well, yes...no...but well, really a *musical* one," Veronica said practically jumping up and down.

Billy stared at her. Waiting.

"My agent just called. Broadway, Billy...Broadway! They're doing a musical version of *The Thin Man* and they want *me*!"

"Let me guess," laughed Peyton Chase as he walked up behind Veronica into the bathroom. "They want to cast you as Asta."

"Hey, hey, hey!" shouted Billy, as he reached into the water to cover his private parts. "Privacy, people. Privacy. Jesus! Can't a guy get a little privacy around here?"

"Oh, calm down, buddy," laughed Peyton. "We've both seen you naked. No big deal."

Veronica snickered.

"It's going to be called *Nick & Nora* and they aren't even going to audition any other actresses. It's being written especially for me. I can't wait!"

"That's great news and I am really *very* proud of you, Ronnie. Honestly. And I am really and truly very, *very* excited. Now if you both will back quietly out of the room and close the door behind you…"

"You'll pleasure yourself?" laughed Peyton.

"Stop it, asshole," shot Billy.

"Let's go into Manhattan tomorrow night to celebrate, Billy," smiled Veronica. "I know just the place."

48

Closing time at The Holly Bush, Devon Stone's favorite pub. He downed the remaining dregs of his drink, stood up putting on his stylish Trilby hat and tipped it to the ruddy-faced young barman.

"God save the queen, Toby," he said as he headed for the door.

"God save the queen, Mr. Stone," the barman replied with a wave of his hand and a bit of a salute. "May she reign as long as Victoria."

"Or longer, Toby. Or longer."

Devon stepped out into the misty, foggy evening. Following the events of the past year, he had become more cautious of his surroundings. Listening for footsteps behind him or looking for assassins hiding in the bushes or behind trees. He was uncomfortable with this new awareness or, more precisely, the need for it. But he hoped to have several more books ahead to write and he felt that he was getting too old for this real-life murder stuff. He would soon put the traumatic events of the past few weeks behind him. His book tour in the "colonies" was about to begin in early August and he once again looked forward to greeting his faithful readers across the pond.

But tonight he was feeling lonely and a bit wistful.

He had had several romantic interludes throughout the years but none of the young ladies (a few of whom were married at the time) had stayed within his heart for too long. For the first time in his life, though, he had recently fallen in love. Really fallen in love. But it was not to be. He knew that Veronica Barron was better suited for her young hero, Billy Bennett. He let out a long sigh as he casually strolled back home.

Although he had seen it on opening night, perhaps tomorrow night he'd go back to see his friend Agatha Christie's *The Mousetrap* again. He never, ever would tell her that he had guessed the killer even before the second act. He was that kind of friend.

49

Vincent Sardi, Jr. lit up like the lights of Times Square when he saw Veronica and Billy enter his restaurant. He said his polite farewell to the guests with whom he was speaking at the time and raced toward Veronica with outstretched arms. He took hold of her hand with both of his and kissed her on both cheeks.

"My dear, dear Veronica Barron," he gushed. "I am beside myself. Walter Winchell simply could not wait to tell me the news."

"Hello, Vince," Veronica responded warmly. "Winchell probably knew about it before I did! I'm pretty excited about it myself."

"And is this your handsome costar?" Sardi asked, smiling at Billy.

Veronica couldn't help but laugh loudly, tossing back her head when she did so. Billy snickered.

"Well, in a manner of speaking, he is, Vince. Vincent Sardi, please say hello to my very best friend, Billy Bennett. A war hero and my savior."

Billy blushed as Vincent shook his hand heartily. He winced a bit because of his bruised knuckles.

"Welcome, then, young man. We both now are in the company of the most beautiful woman soon to be back on Broadway."

Vincent took her hand again and led them both to a table in the center of the main dining room. A table whose occupants were sure to be seen and, at least one of them, possibly recognized by other diners.

"The best seat in the house for you both, my dear," he continued to gush. "And when you have your opening night party here we shall unveil your caricature. I have a spot already selected for it."

"You are way too kind to me, Vince...but don't ever stop!"

And they all laughed.

"I think that was fun," Billy said as he watched Vincent Sardi move on to another table full of guests, "him thinking I was your leading man."

"Put your ego back in your pocket, cowboy," chuckled Veronica. "He knows darn well that Don Ameche has been cast to be my leading man. He was just being his old flattering self."

Billy sighed and leaned forward. He slowly reached into his suit jacket breast pocket.

"Ronnie, I was going to wait until we went up to the top of Rockefeller Plaza after dinner. With all of Manhattan at our feet below and the stars above as our audience, but..."

"Billy," Veronica interrupted with a light turn of her head and a bit of a squint. "I think I've told you in the past that you need a better scriptwriter. I love you to pieces but, honestly, you can lay on the corn a bit thick at times."

"Well, shit," he replied sitting back, only slightly dejected. "I was trying to set a sort of Romeo and Juliet scene, you know...the top of a skyscraper instead of a balcony."

Their waiter approached to take their drink orders.

"Good evening, Miss Barron," he said, bowing slightly. "Welcome back. Oh, and welcome back to Broadway."

"Thank you so much, Peter," answered a gracious Veronica. "It's nice to be back. And it's nice to see you again."

Billy slumped back in his chair as they awaited their cocktails.

"Billy Bennett," said Veronica leaning forward across the table and looking him straight in the eyes. She reached up, grabbing his necktie, and pulled him even closer to her face. "I know that you weren't reaching for your gun in your jacket a few minutes ago. Before I broke the spell. That was *extremely* rude of me and I sincerely apologize. I know that you were about to do something very sweet. Right here in the middle of Sardi's. In front of a theater-going audience. I'm more than flattered. I'm thrilled. And I'm curious."

Billy cocked his head to one side.

"Curious? About what?"

"What the *hell* have you been waiting for? Why have you waited so damn long?"

Billy Bennett laughed so loudly other diners turned to look at him.

"Whatever the question is, Billy, the answer is yes."

Epilogue

Two weeks later…

Six thousand, two hundred and eighty-five miles away, as the crow flies, the ferry captain blew the loud, ear-piercing horn announcing its imminent departure to Papeeté on a sister island across the deep blue sound. A tall young man stood on the bow, his blond hair blowing in the balmy tropical breeze. Two hours before, his friend, one of the wealthy owners of a pineapple plantation on the island, had dropped him off on Mo'ore'a after his long flight and subsequent sailings from Australia.

Twenty minutes later, as the sun was sinking and casting purple, mauve, and cotton candy-pink colors through the scattered clouds above, he walked with a purpose and a noticeable limp toward the Yellow Lizard Gallery. He stopped momentarily before entering to tie a bright red bandana around his neck and to unbutton, halfway, his wrinkled khaki shirt.

The owner of the gallery gasped when she saw him and came running toward him, embracing him warmly.

"Oh, my young Gauguin, you *have* returned! Where have you been all this time? Mr. Tuttle, you're a very, *very* bad boy. I have been so worried about you."

Stepping back, she folded her arms across her chest and tapped her foot like a scolding mother might.

Alistair Stickle smiled broadly; ready to plant the most sensuous, ardent kiss of his life on her lips.

"Martine," he began, "I have a confession to make."

After which, the postponed pleasure from that sunny afternoon many weeks ago began. And continued until daybreak.

Author's Notes

Although it sounds farfetched and something a screenwriter or an author on cannabis would concoct, the Ghost Army actually *did* exist during World War II. Their story was a well-kept secret following the war until it was declassified in 1996. There have been several films and documentaries about this amazing and effective mission. Several of these soldiers/artists went on to make their marks in the art world following the war, including fashion designer Bill Blass, wildlife artist Arthur Singer, and the artist/musician photographer Art Kane.

On February 2, 2022 President Joe Biden signed the "Ghost Army Congressional Gold Medal Act" into law. Thus awarding the members of the Ghost Army the prestigious medal and finally giving them recognition for their unique and highly distinguished service in conducting deception operations in Europe during World War II.

In chapter one, Devon Stone and Brenda Barratt made a brief reference to the renowned "Roundtable" at the Algonquin Hotel.

The Algonquin Round Table was a fabled group of writers, critics, and actors who met for luncheon every single day from 1919 until about 1929. They often referred to themselves as *The Vicious Circle*. They chatted, gossiped, criticized, and drank. And drank some more. They would play witty word games and spout repartee that would make history. Dorothy Parker's famed quote, *"You can lead a horticulture but you can't make her think"* was spawned from one of those games at the Round Table. Harpo Marx was one of the regular attendees but the gathering put off his brother, Groucho. He claimed that the price of admission was a serpent's tongue and a half-concealed stiletto.

While the paintings done by Matteo Amato mentioned in this book are purely fictitious, the subject matter of a couple of them, the *Avenue of Death*, really existed in Manhattan during the late 1800s into the early 1900s. There were *two* avenues, actually. On the west side of the city railroad tracks ran along 10th Avenue and 11th Avenue. They carried commodities such as produce, dairy products, beef, and coal. The trains competed for occupancy on the streets with automobiles, horse and buggies, trucks, and pedestrians. Even with the "West Side Cowboys", men on horseback who rode ahead of the trains waving red flags in warning, there were so many accidents and deaths that the area received its morbid nickname. It has been estimated that there were 548 deaths and 1,574 injuries over the years along 11th Avenue. The West Side Elevated Highway, constructed between 1922 and 1930, eliminated the dreaded Avenues of Death.

A West Side Cowboy

While now obscure and probably hardly noticed, there is a plaque on the wall of an old brick building commemorating this historic, albeit deadly section of the city. The building, currently an upscale, trendy restaurant and brewery, is at 10th Avenue and 29th Street, and the eatery has the unappetizing name Death Avenue.

Circa. 1898
These old bricks and beams will never forget...
The purpose of the High-line and why 10th Avenue
was once nicknamed "Death Avenue"

In memory of the hundreds of people killed by
freight-liners on 10th Ave between 1846 and 1941

The photos that I have used depicting the Avenue of Death were gleaned from the website www.thehighline.org detailing the history of Death Avenue. Fascinating, frightening reading.

Automobile Trivia: Among the popular automobiles (or horseless carriages) of 1903 were the Ford Model A, Benz Parsifal, Mercedes Rennwagen, and even the Cadillac Touring. The United States overtook France in 1904 as the leading car manufacturer in the world not only by volume but also by value. It might be laughable now, but in 1903 there were only 11,235 passenger cars built in the U.S. Ready for another chuckle? The average top speed for cars in 1903 was 28 mph. The base price for a brand new Ford Model A in 1903 was a whopping $850.00.

A Silly Piece of Automobile Trivia: in 1905 there were only two cars in the entire state of Ohio.

They collided.

If any of you may have a question concerning the appraisal of the painting *Memento Mori* in this book for the "staggering sum of $1,000,000", I shall clarify the situation. We all hear of the humongous amounts paid at auction houses for artwork around the globe these days. Countless millions of dollars. The recent sale of a work by Andy Warhol, a silkscreen portrait of Marilyn Monroe, fetched the record-breaking price of $195,000,000, for example. Remember that *this* story takes place in 1953. To put this into perspective, the median annual income for men was estimated at $3,200. For women the sum was $1,200. The sum of $1,000,000 in 1953 would be the equivalent, in today's money, of $10,947,415.73. Enough to kill for?

To all my theater-loving fact-checkers, there actually *was* a musical on Broadway based upon the characters in *The Thin Man* called, oddly enough, *Nick & Nora*. It starred Barry Bostwick and Joanna Gleason. It opened on December 8, 1991, got disastrous, scathing reviews, and closed after nine performances. Murdered by the critics.

The character in this book, Bankston Bruin, Devon Stone's American publisher, would be happy to know that little stuffed toy King Kong gorillas *are* being sold in the gift shop in the lobby of the Empire State Building. Human nature and curiosity, indeed! Not to mention commercialism.

Devon Stone would be thrilled to know that countless thousands of Londoners rejoiced in an elaborate Platinum Jubilee. On June 2, 2022 a spry, 96-year-old Queen Elizabeth II celebrated her historic 70-year reign, bettering Queen Victoria's reign of 63 years. God Save the Queen!

And just in case you might be wondering about that very special dish that Devon Stone requested at Sallie's Bella Luna Trattoria, don't bother Googling it. Just for the fun of it I made up that name but my wife and I have enjoyed a very *real* recipe that could just possibly fit the bill. Buon appetito!

Fettuccine Cipolle e Pancetta

INGREDIENTS

¼ cup olive oil

1 large onion, halved and thinly sliced

1 pound smoked bacon, cut crosswise into ¼" strips

1 bay leaf

¾ cup dry white wine

¾ cup diced canned (or fresh) tomatoes

½ cup chicken broth

1-teaspoon oregano

1-teaspoon red pepper flakes

½ cup Parmigiano-Reggiano, freshly grated

16 ounces fettuccine

INSTRUCTIONS (Yields 4 Servings)

1. In a medium-sized saucepan, sauté the onion slices in the olive oil until soft and translucent, and then set the onions aside. In the same pan, fry the bacon with the bay leaf until the bacon is brown but not crispy. Set aside. Pour off most, but not all of the bacon fat.

2. Add back a small amount of the onions and the white wine, and let simmer for a few minutes. Add the tomatoes, chicken broth, oregano, and the pepper flakes. Stir and let simmer for another ten minutes. If the sauce is drying out, you might want to add just a little bit more of the chicken broth. Meanwhile, cook the fettuccine. Toss the sauce with the fettuccine and the grated Parmigiano-Reggiano, then serve, spooning the bacon and the reserved onions onto the top of each plate.

Acknowledgements

"Everyone is a potential murderer. In everyone there arises from time to time the wish to kill, though not the will to kill."

AGATHA CHRISTIE

As with my four previous books, I have to give high praise (and an occasional low grumble) to my wife of 58 years. Gaylin and I have known each other since we first met in high school when we were naïve teenagers of 15. She has always been my staunchest supporter and the severest of critics. And criticism has been sharp. Just like my lovable character Peyton Chase in this book, Gaylin and our two sons, Gregory and Christopher, speak fluent sarcasm. I have felt their verbal barbs throughout the years but persevered anyway. That's what love is.

I must acknowledge, once again, two of my three handsome grandsons. I usurped their first and middle names respectively for two of my main characters. Needless to say, as intelligent and beguiling as they both are, neither grandson resembles my characters' traits, actions, or appearances in any way. That being said, grandson Peyton actually *is* a pilot.

Devon Stone Hasbrouck

Peyton Chase Hasbrouck

And a great big thank you to my growing list of readers. The joy and satisfaction that I have gotten from being asked to speak at local book clubs has boosted my ego and given me encouragement that my love for writing this late in my life might actually be appreciated by those other than myself.

Printed in the United States
by Baker & Taylor Publisher Services